THE CHRISTMAS VIGIL

A Munro Family
Series Novella

CHRIS TAYLOR

LCT Productions Pty Ltd
18364 Kamilaroi Highway, Narrabri NSW 2390

ISBN: 978-1-925119-17-6 (Print)

The Christmas Vigil is a work of fiction. Names, characters, places, brands, media and incidents either are the product of the author's imagination or are used fictitiously. Any resemblance to actual persons, living or dead, events, or locales, is entirely coincidental.

Published in the United States of America

When former New South Wales District Court judge, **Duncan Munro**, is found lying unconscious in a hotel room surrounded by evidence incriminating him in an affair, his close knit family are rocked to their core.

Marguerite Munro is unwilling to believe her husband of forty years has been cheating on her, but the evidence doesn't lie. Roses, champagne, massage oils, lingerie...it's obvious he was expecting a woman and she knows darn well it wasn't her.

When the distress call goes around the family, they gather together in shock and disbelief. No one wants to believe their father is an adulterer, but the Munro siblings have law enforcement running through their veins. They've learned to look at the facts and draw logical conclusions and all of the evidence is pointing toward their father's guilt...

Will Duncan regain consciousness and provide the explanation they're praying for, or will this be the end of Marguerite's marriage and the Munro family as we know it...?

THE MUNRO FAMILY SERIES

THE PROFILER
(Book One—Clayton and Ellie)

THE INVESTIGATOR
(Book Two—Riley and Kate)

THE PREDATOR
(Book Three—Brandon and Alex)

THE BETRAYAL
(Book Four—Declan and Chloe)

THE DECEPTION
(Book Five—Will and Savannah)

THE NEGOTIATOR
(Book Six—Andy and Cally)

THE CHRISTMAS VIGIL
(A Munro Family Series Novella)

THE RANSOM
(Book Seven—Lane and Zara)

THE DEFENDANT
(Book Eight—Chase and Josie)

THE SHOOTING
(Book Nine—Tom and Lily)

THE MAKER
(Book Ten—Bryce and Chanel)

DEDICATION

This book is dedicated to my mother, Sophia Guihot
and to my mother-in-law, Gloria Wilde:
for all that you are and all that you do, I love you.

And, as always, to my gorgeous husband, Linden,
who has my heart 'til death do us part.

THE CHRISTMAS VIGIL

CHAPTER 1

Duncan
Grafton, New South Wales

Former New South Wales District Court judge, Duncan Munro pushed the card into the required slot and opened the door to the hotel room. Checking left and right to make sure the way was clear, he slipped inside. The door clicked shut behind him and his breath caught on a pleased sigh.

The desk clerk had outdone herself. It must have been the friendly wink he'd given her when he asked for their best room. Either that, or the fifty-dollar bill he'd tucked under the registration form had done the trick. The suite was large and spacious, with floor-to-ceiling glass framing the view of the gloriously wide Clarence River. The salt-water river fed into the Pacific Ocean about thirty miles away and left the water a clean dark blue. It sparkled in the early afternoon sunlight and sent shards of diamonds reaching for the sky. He'd lived in the area for nearly forty years and yet he never tired of looking at it. Today, the brightness hurt his eyes.

He turned away and pinched the bridge of his nose in an effort to assuage the pain. Now wasn't the time to feel unwell. Not when he had so much to do before she arrived. With that thought in mind, he picked up the small suitcase he'd left by the door and carried it over to the king-sized bed.

The sight of the pristine white bedspread gave him pause. His wife would have a fit if she saw him place the old suitcase on top of it. But she wasn't here and she'd never know. Besides, it would be easier and quicker for him to prepare the room this way.

His belly tightened with excitement at the thought of what lay ahead. He'd been planning it for weeks, right down to the last, infinitesimal detail. Finally, the day had arrived.

And here he was.

With hands that were less than steady, he unzipped the suitcase and lifted the lid. He stared down at the contents and his heart skipped a beat. Blood rushed to his groin and his cock stirred. Reaching into the suitcase, he pulled out the black satin and lace negligee. He caressed it in his hands and rubbed the softness of it against his cheek. 'One size fits all,' the salesgirl had assured him. He hoped so. He couldn't wait to see her in it.

A fresh wave of excitement surged through him. She'd probably be a little shy, but that was okay. He'd coax her into wearing it and she'd eventually put it on because she wanted more than anything to please him. And she would. *Oh yes, she would.*

A groan escaped at the thought of the hours that lay ahead—hours he would spend traversing every inch of her body with his hands and his mouth and his tongue. His cock, already rock-hard, would find her wetness and he'd fuck her until they both lay limp and exhausted. The thought of it was almost too much to bear.

His hand strayed to his erection and he rubbed it through his shorts. The urge to pop the button and slide down the zip was almost overwhelming, but he resisted. It wasn't fair to either of them to start without her. Besides, keeping his desire at a fever pitch until she came would make it better for both of them.

Returning his attention to the contents of the suitcase, he set out the negligee carefully, almost reverently, across the bedspread. She'd see it the moment she walked in. It was how he'd planned it. His gaze fell on the red velvet jeweller's case which lay in the suitcase—another surprise he knew she would love.

He opened the case and stared down at the necklace. The brilliant blue sapphires, blood-red rubies and clear white diamonds sparkled almost as bright as the river. It was a beautiful piece and had set him back a fortune, but the moment he spotted it in the window, he'd known it was perfect.

Striding over to the nightstand nearest the window, he opened the drawer and slipped the case inside. That surprise was for later. He couldn't wait to show her. He glanced at his watch and noted the time. The minutes had slipped away.

Working more quickly now, he emptied the suitcase of lubricant and massage oils and arranged them on the nightstand. He wanted them close at hand. Next, he removed a dozen fat candles. Some were short and others were taller. The girl in the shop had assured him they all smelled delicious and would burn for at least six hours.

More than enough time.

He scattered the candles around the room in groups of three and four, taking care not to leave them too close to the drapes. It wouldn't do to set the place on fire—that was a sure way to send his plans awry. Feeling in his pocket for his lighter, he frowned, remembering too late he'd given the cigarettes away. He'd finally given in to his wife's urgings to put a little more effort into his health and as a result, he no longer had a need for a lighter.

He'd have to request one from housekeeping and make sure it arrived before she did. She wasn't expecting his call and he had no idea where she was, but she'd come when he asked. Of that, he had no doubt.

He strode over to the telephone that sat on the desk on the other side of the room. Picking up the receiver, he rubbed absently at the pain that continued to niggle behind his eyes. His vision blurred and he blinked to clear it.

The call connected and his thoughts were diverted. He

requested a lighter be brought to his suite and then asked to be transferred to room service. He was always famished after sex and so was she.

He placed an order for the two of them and asked for the delivery to be delayed. After confirming a bottle of Moët and two champagne glasses would be brought to his suite directly, he hung up the phone and returned to the bed where he removed the final item from the suitcase: A single, perfect red rose.

He brought it up to his face and inhaled its fragrance. Heady and sweet, it was everything he hoped for. He closed his eyes and luxuriated in the whisper soft stroke of the velvet petals across his mouth and imagined her lips in their place.

Soon, very soon.

With a last caress of its petals, he placed the rose on the pillow. Shutting the lid on the empty suitcase, he fastened the zip before carrying it across the room and stowing it in the closet. Returning to the bed, he smoothed out the wrinkles on the bedspread and then stood back to survey the results.

It was perfect, just like he'd imagined. All that was missing was her.

A knock on the door interrupted his musings and he strode across to open it. A young bellboy offered him a smile in greeting and wheeled in a small table covered in a white linen cloth. The boy's gaze strayed to the bed and his eyes widened in surprise. He glanced at Duncan with a knowing grin.

Duncan raised an eyebrow and wordlessly dared the boy to comment, but the boy's gaze fell to the floor and he wisely chose to remain silent. Someone had trained him well. An ice bucket containing the unopened champagne and a couple of crystal glasses stood on the table. A lighter lay to one side.

Duncan nodded his approval and went to reach for his wallet. Too late, he remembered he'd left it locked in the glove compartment of his car. Not that it mattered in Australia where tips were neither necessary nor expected.

"You let me know if there's anything else you need, Mr Smith," the boy said. "Just ask for Charlie."

"Thank you, Charlie. I'll be sure to do that." After closing the door, Duncan returned to the table. He lifted the champagne out of its frozen bath and smiled in satisfaction. The bottle was icy cold. Everything was ready.

It was time to call her.

Sudden nerves of anticipation coursed through his arteries and tightened his gut. He'd waited so long and now the moment was almost upon him. He tugged out his phone and then gasped in agony. Pain like he'd never known seared through his head and burst behind his eyes in white-hot shards of torture. He clutched at his face in an effort to stem it and stumbled toward the bed. The phone fell from his fingers and landed, unnoticed, on the carpet.

Groaning and holding his head in his hands, he collapsed onto the bedspread and curled up in a ball. The headache was beyond excruciating. He gasped on a sob and tears leaked from his scrunched-up eyes. He couldn't bear to open them. His head was going to burst.

Nausea gripped his belly and he doubled over again. In some distant part of his brain, he knew he had to get to the bathroom, but the signals to his legs just weren't getting through. His stomach cramped and tightened and vomit spewed from his mouth. It dripped down the side of the pristine white bedspread. He stared at the mess in horror and disappointment until everything turned to black…

CHAPTER 2

Marguerite
Grafton, New South Wales

Marguerite Munro gazed at her reflection in the mirror and smiled up at her hairdresser.

"What are you up to for Christmas, Shelley? It isn't far away."

The young hairdresser grinned. "You're right. It's less than a week away and I still haven't done any shopping. I'm hopeless. Every year, I vow I'll be more organized next time, but it never seems to happen."

Marguerite laughed softly. "You're lucky you don't have too many to buy for. Me, I have to start in June if I'm going to have any chance of finding gifts for everyone."

"Yes, I can well understand that. You have the largest family I know. Are they all coming home for Christmas?"

"I hope so. Riley and Kate will be here, of course. They live not far away. Chanel will be on Christmas break from university and Josie has the time off work. I'm hoping the other boys will make it. I love it when we're all together. I haven't seen some of them for a while."

Shelley completed the finishing touches to her hair and stood back with a mirror to give Marguerite a view from the back.

"There you are, Mrs Munro. All done."

"Thank you, Shelley. You've done a wonderful job, as usual. Grafton's lucky to have stolen you away from the city. I don't know how you manage to keep weaving your magic on an old woman like me."

Shelley smiled with genuine affection. "Now, listen here, Mrs Munro, I refuse to listen to another word about you being old. You're...*mature*, that's all and the way you look, you'd give women half your age a run for their money. I might add a touch-up here and the odd highlight there, but you're the one with the goods. Your hair is thicker than some thirty-year-olds and that color...all that gold and honey and wheat. You can't get that kind of combination out of a bottle."

Marguerite smiled back at her and patted the girl's hand in gratitude. Marguerite was old enough to be her grandmother, but she appreciated the sentiment and the kindness that shone from the young girl's eyes.

"Well, whatever it is, I'm grateful," Marguerite replied. "I always feel like a million dollars when I walk out of here and my hair simply never looks better."

Shelley smiled again and helped her out of her chair. Collecting her handbag from where she'd left it near her feet, Marguerite moved over to the counter and fished inside for her purse. Her phone vibrated against her hand. She'd turned it on silent when she arrived, refusing to allow anything to interrupt the couple of hours of bliss she enjoyed every six weeks at the salon.

Tugging it out of her handbag, she glanced at the screen. Her breath caught. Nine missed calls. *Nine*. How could that be?

Sudden fear crawled insidiously along her spine and dread tightened her stomach. Nothing about nine missed calls could be good. It was as simple as that. Something had happened. Her thoughts immediately flew to her family.

"Are you all right, Mrs Munro? You've gone very pale."

She did her best to focus on Shelley, who now frowned at her in concern. Marguerite reached out and grabbed the counter in an effort to steady herself. "Yes, yes of course," she managed and hurriedly paid her bill. "K-keep the change, Shelley. I'll see you again soon."

"We haven't made your next appointment, Mrs Munro. Would you like me to—?"

Marguerite let the door to the salon close behind her, cutting off the rest of Shelley's question. She hadn't meant to be rude, but she didn't have time to make another appointment. She had to find out what was wrong.

With shaking hands, she pulled her phone out again and stared hard at the screen. Two of the calls were from the same number, a number she didn't recognize. The others were from her son, Riley. The screen indicated she had three new voice messages. She dialed into her voicemail, her breath coming fast.

The first message was from a Detective Joel Parker from the Grafton Police Station who urged her to call him back as *soon as she could.* He sounded solemn and the quiet urgency in his voice terrified her.

She listened to the remaining two messages, both from Riley. He lived closest to her than any of her children and was her fourth-born son. *Well, kind of fourth.* Riley was a twin, but he'd been born first. There were only three minutes and forty-five seconds between him and his brother, a fact Clayton, Riley's twin, took immense delight in frequently reminding him, particularly now the pair of them had dropped over the other side of thirty. In fact, they were nearly thirty-three.

Where had the time gone…?

She shook her head and tried to concentrate on Riley's messages. They were short and succinct. They told her nothing.

Mom, as soon as you get this message, please call me.

Mom, you need to call me.

Mom, where are you?

His tone was increasingly desperate, but it was his lack of information that filled her with dread. That, and the way he spoke. He'd used his police voice. The one he used when he was addressing the thirty or so officers under his command; the tone that brooked no argument.

With panic nipping at the edges of her consciousness, Marguerite stumbled to a nearby bus shelter and took refuge from the summer heat. Ignoring the startled look from a waiting passenger, she dropped clumsily to the low steel bench and fumbled with her phone. She had to call Riley. She had to find out what had happened.

With shaking hands, she dialed his number and waited for the call to connect. He answered immediately.

"Mom, thank God. Where have you been? I've been trying to call you!"

"Wh-what's wrong?" she stammered, her lips so dry she could barely form the words.

Riley paused. "It's…it's Dad. He's suffered a brain hemorrhage, or something. They've taken him straight to the operating theater."

Fear held Marguerite frozen. "Wh-when?" she managed.

"About an hour ago. I've been trying to get hold of you."

Guilt surged through her and she bit her lip against the pain. Her husband had been hurting, possibly dying while she'd been blissfully unaware, enjoying being pampered by her hairdresser, content to switch her phone to silent and block out the rest of the world.

"H-how is he?"

Riley blew out his breath on a heavy sigh and the fear inside her magnified. *Oh, heavens. Was she too late? Please, God, don't let her be too late…*

"I don't know, Mom. He's still in surgery. He was unconscious when they found him."

"Oh, dear Lord!" she cried out in distress and jammed her fist against her mouth, as if she could somehow hold the pain in. The waiting passenger sidled away, shaking his head at her and muttering under his breath. She barely noticed.

"I'm at the hospital now. I'm waiting for the doctor to get out of surgery and tell me what the hell's going on."

"Who…who found him?" All she could picture was her husband lying unconscious, alone and in pain, tending the roses in the back garden, where she'd last seen him a mere handful of hours ago.

Riley remained silent. Marguerite frowned. "Riley, what's the matter? Where was he? Who found him?"

"Mom, it doesn't matter. Just come to the hospital. You need to come. Please."

Riley ended the call and Marguerite stared at the phone in bewilderment. *Why hadn't he answered her questions?* Confused and disorientated and weighed down with dread, she stared blindly around her and did her best to tamp down her panic. *Where had she parked her car?* For the life of her, she couldn't remember.

The salon was halfway along the main street. Surrounded by other shops, it was always difficult to find a parking spot, especially around lunchtime and with the streets full of Christmas shoppers. She gazed blindly at the cars that lined the street, but none of them were familiar.

She shook her head and tried to slow her breathing. *She was being silly.* The car had to be somewhere nearby. Ignoring her growing anxiety, she tossed her phone into her handbag and stood a little unsteadily. She stumbled out of the bus shelter and headed in the direction of the mall. Sometimes she would park in the underground car park there. It kept the worst of the summer heat out of the vehicle and even though it was a little further away, there was always a better chance of finding a vacant car space. *Perhaps that's where she left her vehicle?*

Her recent conversation with Riley replayed in her head and she frowned again. *What wasn't he telling her?* And why the call from Detective Parker? Why would the *police* be involved? She knew she should simply pick up her phone, return the detective's call and find out exactly what was going on, but try as she might, she couldn't do it. Fear of what she might discover held her back. A deep sense of foreboding took hold of her and wouldn't let her go.

Her body trembled. The cacophony of noise from passing cars and pedestrians echoed in her head. She spun around, looking both left and right. Her gaze bounced wildly from the people around her, going about their business, oblivious to her turmoil and confusion.

She stepped off the sidewalk and was immediately blasted by a car horn. She jumped back and narrowly avoided being hit. She stumbled and almost fell.

This was madness.

She didn't even know what the problem was—or even if there *was* a problem. Her husband had suffered a brain hemorrhage, but he was still alive. Her son had been sketchy on the details. That was all. There was no reason for her to turn the situation into a drama of mindless proportions with no good reason. She had to get a grip, calm down. She had to find her car and head over to the hospital, to Duncan and to Riley.

Riley. He was waiting for her. He'd make everything all right. He always did. As the only one of her seven children who had returned to live nearby, she'd come to depend upon him more and more over the years and was genuinely fond of his lovely wife, Kate. And then there were their children, her grandbabies. The twins, Rosie and Daisy were two-and-a-half years old and were growing cheekier by the day. They called her 'gran' and offered her toothy smiles while they plastered her with sticky kisses. She loved every minute of it.

Of course, they weren't her only grandchildren. All five of her sons had offspring. It was only the youngest of her children, her daughters, Josie and Chanel, who were yet to marry and produce grandbabies. Between the five boys, she had ten grandchildren and each and every one of them was dear to her heart. It was just that Riley was the only one close at hand and his toddlers the only ones she saw regularly.

Thinking of her family, her breathing slowed until at last, it was almost regular. The distraction had done her good and little by little, she clawed back her self-control. She'd always prided herself on being cool and collected—in fact, in her nursing days, she'd been renowned for it. She hadn't managed to work for several years in busy trauma units without knowing how to remain calm in a crisis. Yet, here she was, on the verge of falling apart in the middle of the afternoon on a public street and she still didn't know what had happened.

Duncan was unconscious. Okay, she could deal with that. Unconscious wasn't dead. Unconscious could mean anything. Who knows? He may even now be waking up.

With that thought in mind, she blinked hard to clear her vision and drew in another deep breath. Squaring her shoulders, she made a more concerted effort to locate her car. A minute later, she spotted it, parked near the escalators that took shoppers into the mall. Hurrying over to it, she dug in her handbag for her keys and breathed a sigh of relief when her fingers closed around them. The hospital was in another part of town, well away from the main street. All of a sudden, she couldn't get there quickly enough.

CHAPTER 3

Marguerite
Grafton Base Hospital

Marguerite hurried into the lobby of the Grafton Base Hospital, barely noticing the brightly colored Christmas decorations that hung from the ceiling. She headed straight for the information desk. While she'd never worked there, she knew the hospital well. She volunteered three times a week in the hospital cafeteria. She was a familiar sight on the grounds. The girl manning the desk wore a cheerful Santa hat and smiled upon her approach.

"Mrs Munro, how are you today? Might I say, your hair looks spectacular. I wish I could get that kind of color. Where do you get—"

Marguerite's smile was strained. "Isabelle, sweetheart, thank you, but I'm in a bit of a rush. My husband's been admitted to the hospital. Could you please tell me where I can find him?"

Isabelle's face collapsed in shock and embarrassment. "Oh, I'm so sorry! I didn't realize. I'll let you know in just a minute." The girl quickly tapped on the keyboard in front of her and focused on the computer screen. A moment later, she bit her lip and a frown appeared between her eyes. She looked up and met Marguerite's anxious gaze.

"I'm sorry, Mrs Munro, he's in the Intensive Care Unit. It's up on level three."

Marguerite's her heart plummeted at the news. Only the sickest patients were treated in the ICU. Refusing to let the knowledge affect her, she nodded her thanks to Isabelle and headed toward the elevators.

Much too soon or way too long, the elevator *dinged* and opened its doors. She drew in a deep breath and stepped into the quiet corridor. Riley sat hunched in a hard plastic chair outside the door to the ICU. He looked up at her approach. For a moment, relief flooded his face and eased a little of the tension that held his jaw tight. He stood when she reached him and engulfed her in a hug that was tinged with desperation.

"Thank Christ. I'm so glad you're here, Mom."

Marguerite nodded and pulled out of his arms. "How is he?"

Riley's shoulders slumped. "He's out of surgery, but still unconscious. The doctor came out awhile ago and told me a blood vessel at the base of Dad's brain has ruptured. They've repaired the damage to the vein, but only time will tell how much damage his brain's suffered."

Her stomach took a dive. "Have you seen him?"

"Not yet. I was out on a job when I took the call from Joel Parker. He's the detective who attended the scene. He recognized Dad right away. He'd tried to call you, but you didn't answer."

"Yes, he left a message on my phone." Marguerite reflexively touched her freshly cut, dyed and blow-waved hair. "I-I was at Shelley's salon."

Riley nodded brusquely. "When Joel couldn't reach you, he called me."

"Of course. I'm glad he did." She paused, still trying to piece everything together. "Why were the police notified? Where in heaven's name was he found?"

Riley averted his gaze. A blush stained his cheeks. Marguerite stared at him, her instincts on high alert. *What wasn't he telling her?* The dread that had eased slightly upon her arrival at the hospital now returned in full force.

"What is it, Riley? What aren't you telling me?"

He met her gaze without flinching, but the tension in his jaw told her how much of an effort it was. She held her breath, instinctively knowing something was terribly wrong.

"They...they found him unconscious in a hotel room near the river."

"A *hotel* room? What on earth are you talking about? That can't possibly be right. What would your father be doing in a hotel room? I saw him at home in the garden not long before I left for my appointment."

Riley's cheeks turned redder and he once again averted his gaze. Her dread escalated into full blown confusion, holding her immobile. She stared at her son, unblinking and unmoving and willed him to provide a logical explanation.

"J-Joel says it appears that Dad was..." His voice faded away.

Impatience and an increasing anxiety made her voice sharp. "For heaven's sake, Riley, spit it out. Why was your father in a hotel room?"

Riley closed his eyes and drew in a deep breath, his face pained. Marguerite bit her lip until she tasted blood, suddenly sure she didn't want to know. Before she could tell Riley she'd changed her mind, he spoke in a voice that was rough with shock and disbelief.

"Joel attended the scene. He said it appears Dad was at the hotel for the purposes of...of a romantic assignation. That he was expecting a woman—"

A low growl of denial started deep in her throat and made its way out through her mouth. Her vision narrowed to mere pinpricks of light and there was a roaring in her ears.

She'd heard him wrong. It couldn't be right. An *affair?* It wasn't possible. Not her husband. Not Duncan. She refused to believe it.

"*No!*" she shook her head from side to side with increasing vehemence. "No, you're wrong. Joel's wrong. Your father would never cheat on me. I won't believe it. You can't make me believe it."

Riley's face filled with sadness and pity. The sight of it infuriated her. "Don't you dare look at me like that, Riley Munro. *Don't you dare*. I don't care what Joel thinks. He's wrong. Do you hear me? He's *wrong*. There's no way your father's having an affair."

"Mom, he was found in a suite at the Bellevue Hotel. He'd registered as John Smith. According to Joel, there was more than one sign that he was expecting company...of the female kind."

Marguerite absorbed the information as best as she could, but the words hammered away in her heart. The Bellevue Hotel was a renowned meeting place for illicit liaisons and why would Duncan give a false name? *Why would he be there at all?* It didn't make sense. None of it did.

"I want to see him," she demanded. "I won't believe it until he tells me himself and even then, I might not believe it."

Riley shook his head. "Oh, Mom. I know how you feel. I feel the same way. Dad, an adulterer? I can't believe it, either. I don't want to believe it. But the facts don't lie." He drew in a ragged breath and looked away. When his gaze returned to hers, she almost gasped at the bleakness in his eyes.

"I didn't want to tell you, Mom, but I think you need to know. Joel found a rose and a piece of racy lingerie on the bed. The receipt for the clothing was in Dad's luggage. Two hundred and fifty dollars and it was only dated a week day ago. There was lubricant and massage oil on the nightstand. He'd ordered expensive champagne and two glasses—"

"Noooo!" She put her hands over her ears, unable to bear listening to any more. Her jaw was clenched so tight, she thought her teeth might snap. The sob worked its way up through the tension in her stomach, the constriction in her chest, until at last, she couldn't hold it back.

She howled. Her breath came fast. Riley stepped forward, pleading and placating. He tried to hold her, but she pushed him away.

It wasn't true. It couldn't be true. The police had it wrong. Duncan wouldn't cheat on her. It would be more likely for him to fly to the moon. They'd been married forty years. Only that morning, he'd kissed her good-bye and told her how much he loved her.

It was a lie. It was all a lie. She needed to see him, to speak with him. She needed to hear him tell her it wasn't true. She refused to believe every word, every smile, every kiss—forty years of togetherness—had been a lie. She refused to believe her life and their love had been nothing more than an illusion.

Spinning on her heel, she strode over to the door of the ICU and stabbed at the buzzer. The intercom crackled and was answered by someone almost immediately. Marguerite cleared her throat and straightened her shoulders and requested entry to see her husband.

A few moments later, the door was opened from the inside and a young nurse with blond hair and kind blue eyes greeted them quietly.

"H-how is he?" Marguerite stammered, fear now constricting her throat. She was grateful for Riley's presence.

"He's still unconscious, but he's doing okay," the nurse replied, directing her response to Marguerite. "The doctors are pleased with the way he came through the surgery. We'll know more soon. You can come in and see him, if you like."

Marguerite nodded and glanced behind her to where Riley stood, tense and still. The nurse followed her gaze.

"I'm sorry, but the doctors have restricted his visitors to one at a time and for only a few minutes each. It's tiring for the patient, regardless of their level of consciousness."

Riley gave a brief nod and stepped back. "Of course. I understand. I'll wait for you out here, Mom."

Marguerite acknowledged him with the slightest movement of her head, her focus now entirely on the hospital ward. In a matter of moments, she'd see her husband—not as she had a matter of hours ago, but gravely ill, unconscious… She steeled herself against the impact and followed the nurse through the ward.

CHAPTER 4

Riley
Watervale, New South Wales

Riley stared after his mother. He recalled the pain and devastation on her face when he'd first given her the news and then how she'd pulled herself together and marched into the ICU like it was something she did every day. Admiration for her courage and her strength flooded through him and he couldn't help but send a desperate plea heavenwards, that her faith in his father wasn't misplaced.

When Joel had called him with the discovery, he'd refused to believe it. Not his father, the former judge: upstanding, loyal, unimpeachable. It wasn't possible. But the evidence was there for all to see, including Charlie, the boy at the hotel who had raised the alarm.

His father had ordered room service; enough food for two. When Charlie's knock had gone unanswered, he'd become more than a little concerned. He'd spoken to the judge a couple of hours earlier and had noticed...certain things. The boy had alerted the manager who then entered the room by force. Duncan had been found on the bed, unconscious and barely breathing.

With no wallet or ID, and nothing more than the name he'd registered under, the hotel manager had no choice but to call the police. They'd arrived right behind the paramedics. It had taken Joel less than three seconds to realize it was Riley's father.

Riley had jumped into his unmarked squad car and had driven the two hours to Grafton. He'd phoned his wife, Kate, on the way and had stumbled through an explanation. He couldn't even recall what he'd said. He then phoned his mother more times than he could remember and cursed when he kept getting her voice mail.

His mother... He couldn't imagine what she was feeling. He prayed she'd be okay.

Okay? What was he thinking? Of course she wasn't okay. Neither of them were okay and his brothers and sisters wouldn't be, either.

The reminder that his siblings had yet to be informed stopped him cold. *What was he going to tell them?* They respected and adored their father. He'd been a positive role model all of their lives and an inspiration to them all. To be appointed the first aboriginal judge to the New South Wales District Court was an achievement that had left all of them in awe—even more so now that they were adults and could fully appreciate exactly what it had taken Duncan Munro to get there.

Riley drew in a deep breath and tried to ease the tension that gripped his body. Glancing down the corridor, he noticed it was empty and suddenly longed for the comfort of Kate's arms. His stumbled explanation had been met with shock and confusion. He couldn't even remember whether she responded. Of course, she would have. He wished he could remember what she'd said.

The door to the ICU opened and his mother hurried out. Riley stepped forward, but she averted her gaze.

"Mom! How is he?"

She looked up. Tears shimmered in her eyes. Riley's gut clenched at the pain and sadness and deep concern that shadowed their bright blue depths. As if beyond words, she shook her head in silence and rushed past him, headed in the direction of the elevators. A moment later, he heard the elevator *ding* and watched as she stepped inside and disappeared from sight.

A few minutes later, the doctor Riley had briefly spoken to earlier filled the doorway of the ICU and came toward him, his face grim. The fear Riley had done his best to keep at bay for the last hour surged through him.

"Commander Munro," the doctor greeted him.

"Riley. Please, call me Riley."

"Riley." The doctor nodded. "I'm Jordan Holland, one of the ICU registrars. Sorry, I didn't have time to introduce myself earlier. We were a little...busy. I wanted to catch your mother, but she left before I could speak to her. I told you your father's had a ruptured brain aneurysm. I wanted to make sure you understand what that means."

Riley nodded. A block of concrete lodged itself in his gut. He swallowed against the panic and tried to answer. "Isn't that some kind of bleed?"

"Yes. Aneurysms occur when there's a weakness in the artery wall and when they rupture it causes a bleed. They can appear anywhere, but in your father's case, there's been a thinning of the blood vessel near the base of his brain, forming a ballooning where pressure builds. Today, it decided to rupture."

Riley stared at the doctor. He looked about Riley's age. The man sported thick, dark hair that was in need of a cut and looked like he'd run his hand through it more than once. His brown eyes were serious, but Riley saw the kindness in them...and the fatigue. It couldn't be easy working in such a high-risk area of medicine, where life and death often hung in the balance.

Riley closed his eyes and braced himself for what he had to know. A moment later, he opened his eyes and forced the question through his lips. "Is he still alive?"

"Yes, but he remains unconscious. The surgery went well. We located the source of the rupture and have repaired it. We've also managed to stop the bleeding. He's still showing signs of normal brain activity, but at this stage, we can't tell what kind of long-term damage he's sustained, if any. I believe he was unconscious for a couple of hours, maybe more, before he was discovered. We'll just have to wait and see what happens."

"He will wake up, though, won't he?"

The doctor shrugged. "I'd like to hope so, but it's too early to tell. We're going to monitor him closely and see how it goes."

"C-can I see him?" Riley asked.

"Yes, of course, although we're restricting his visitors to one at a time for now and for no more than a few minutes each."

"Thank you. The nurse told us. I promise I won't be long."

The doctor nodded and appeared satisfied with Riley's answer. "Follow me, I'll show you the way."

Within moments, Riley was inside the quiet, sterile environment that was the ICU. The only sounds came from the beeping of the machines that stood beside every patient and the occasional, low murmur of voices from staff. The room was large and open and well lit. Riley supposed that the patients in the beds were mostly unconscious and wouldn't know day from night anyway.

The nurses' station was positioned in the middle of the room and afforded a view of every bed. His father's was the closest.

"He's right here," the doctor said quietly, indicating Riley's father with a slight movement of his head. "I'll leave you with him."

"Thank you," Riley muttered, barely able to concentrate on anything other than the man who lay in the bed. His head was swathed in bandages. Tubes protruded from his arms. Another one went up his nose. A large tube, attached to a respirator, filled his mouth. He was ashen and still. He looked like death had already come to claim him.

Riley stared at the man he loved and admired more than any other and was still shocked by what Joel had told him. He felt just as strongly as his mother that somehow, they'd got it wrong. Despite the evidence pointing to the contrary, it was inconceivable his father could be having an affair.

He clung to his knowledge of the man who laid so deathly pale in the bed. His father was his idol, his inspiration. It had always been that way. Out of all the Munro children, Riley looked the most like his aboriginal father. He'd taken strength and courage from his father's achievements to help him get through the difficult times when schoolyard bullies had been less than kind about the color of his skin.

Now that he was an adult, his bi-racial heritage was no longer an issue, but as a child and a gawky, uncertain teenager, he'd held onto the realization that his father had faced similar challenges, and maybe worse, and had risen far above that. It had given Riley the strength and determination to do the same.

Riley was proud of the man he'd become and of the life he'd made. At thirty, he'd been the youngest ever New South Wales Police Officer to be appointed to the position of Local Area Commander. Three years on and he was the loving husband of his beautiful Kate and the proud father of Daisy and Rosie. The twins were were the center of his world. He couldn't imagine doing anything to hurt them. They were his family; they were his life. And his father would feel the same about them...surely?

The evidence was purely circumstantial and facts could be made to lie. *Couldn't they?* He was a detective, trained to observe and draw logical conclusions from the circumstances in the absence of any other explanation, but he refused to accept there was any truth to his father's infidelity, despite what had been discovered in the hotel.

He thought of his mother's reaction to the news and it pained him anew. It was obvious the woman his father had been expecting wasn't her. The news had blindsided her as much as it had blindsided Riley. *But if not her, then who? And why?*

Renewed despair and frustration rushed through him and he had to turn away. With clenched fists, he tried to breathe through the pain. "You need to wake up, Dad," he gasped. "You need to tell us what happened."

The list of incriminating items found in the hotel room spun madly through his head, over and over in a blur of black and white words until it was all he could do not to cry out. With a ragged breath, he turned back to face the man in the bed, wanting to shake him, to demand answers, to demand the truth. But his father remained unmoved, pasty and still and silent, except for the machines that kept him alive.

A sob escaped Riley's tightly compressed lips. Tears burned behind his eyes. He blinked hard, refusing to let them fall.

"Don't leave us hanging like this, Dad. We need you to wake up. We need you to tell us the truth." With gritted teeth and clenched fists, he stumbled away, unable to stand by another moment. He headed back in what he hoped was the direction he'd entered. Finding the exit, he shouldered the door open.

He staggered into the corridor and gasped in relief to be out of there, away from the sickness, away from the pain, away from the questions that hammered in his head—the questions his father might never get to answer. The phone in his pocket vibrated against his chest and he snatched at it with fingers gone clumsy from shock and from grief. He checked the Caller ID and had to lean against the nearest wall for support.

It was Clayton. His twin.

CHAPTER 5

Clayton

Canberra, Australian Capital Territory

Clayton rubbed at the ache in his shoulder and tried to concentrate on the thick file in front of him. A monster was luring a string of young Canberra girls into their clutches and then savagely beating them to death. As a senior profiler with the Australian Federal Police, he'd been asked to put together a profile of the perpetrator, but try as he might, today his mind wouldn't stay focused.

It might have had something to do with the stupid argument he'd had with his wife, Ellie, that morning or the fact that all three of his young children had been up half the night ill with a virus, but the sense of foreboding had been with him since lunchtime and no matter how hard he tried, he'd been unable to shake it. Giving in to the urge to call his twin, he picked up the phone and dialed Riley's number. It seemed to ring forever before it was eventually answered.

"Hey, Clay, how are you?"

Clayton frowned at Riley's subdued tone. "Not bad, big brother. For a moment there, I didn't think you were going to answer." He stretched out in his chair and stacked his boots on his desk. When his twin didn't reply with his usual quick banter, Clayton's sense of unease went into overdrive. He sat up straight and took a deep breath, refusing to believe it could be anything serious. He was being stupid, overly sensitive and beyond tired. That's all it was.

Despite the silent reassurances, he wasn't convinced. "Talk to me, Riles. What's wrong?"

The silence lengthened. Dread began to form in the pit of Clayton's gut. He heard Riley's quick intake of breath. A moment later, his brother spoke.

"I-I was just about to call you. It's Dad. He...he's been taken to the hospital. He's not good."

Clayton's heart pounded so hard he could barely hear Riley's words. Fear rushed through his veins and dried the saliva in his mouth. He swallowed and tried to speak. "W-what happened?"

"The doctor says he suffered a ruptured brain aneurysm. An artery blew out and caused a bleed. We...we don't know much more than that. He's been unconscious since they brought him in."

"Shit." Clayton shook his head in disbelief. "Is he okay? I mean, he's not going to die or anything, is he?"

"At this point he's in the ICU, recovering from emergency surgery and they don't know anything for sure. He still has normal brain activity, which is a good sign, but we'll have to wait and see."

Images of his father—tall and broad shouldered, a mountain of a man—ran through Clayton's head. Larger than life and fit as a bull, he couldn't imagine him lying sick and helpless—maybe even dying. *No, not dying.* He refused to believe that.

"Where is he?" he asked, instinctively reaching for his keyboard. He needed to book a flight.

"He's at the base hospital in Grafton."

"Where's Mom? She must be going out of her mind. Was she the one who found him?"

Again, the silence stretched between them. A fresh wave of foreboding held Clayton immobile. His fingers froze on the keyboard.

"Riley? Talk to me. Where's Mom? What the fuck's happened?" He couldn't keep the urgency out of his voice, or his escalating fear. His hand clenched the phone so tightly, he was afraid it might snap.

His brother sighed heavily and Clayton's anxiety ratcheted up another notch. Before he could speak again, Riley answered him.

"There's something I haven't told you."

Twenty minutes later, Clayton's mind was still reeling with shock. He'd listened while Riley recounted the events up to the time his father collapsed and he was stunned beyond speech. *It couldn't be true.* No matter what the facts were, it couldn't be true. His parents had been married four decades. They were wholly devoted to each other. It had always been that way.

As a teenager and even as a young adult, he'd sometimes envied their closeness. They were often so totally and completely focused on one another, there were times when it seemed there was no one else but them. It wasn't that he hadn't felt loved. All his life, he'd known that he very much mattered to both of them and with seven loud and rambunctious children in the house, it had taken a couple of very special people to ensure each one of them felt valued. Somehow, his parents had managed it.

His mom and dad understood their children's struggles and had been just as devastated as Clayton had been when he lost his first wife at a young age to suicide. And later, when he found Ellie, the love and support from his parents and their sheer happiness for him had been nearly overwhelming. They were his yardstick for measuring his success—as a husband, as a father, as a friend. Without even being aware of it, even now they pushed him onward and upward, and he was always challenging himself to be the best man he could possibly be.

All his life, he'd aspired to be like them—strong and

determined, kind and compassionate. Born to aboriginal parents, Duncan Munro was proud of his native Australian heritage. Intelligent, charismatic and loyal, there was nothing he couldn't do.

His mother was just as admirable. Born and bred in Sydney, she was the only daughter of wealthy Caucasian parents. Blond and tall and beautiful, she could have been a model. But the inside of her was just as beautiful as the outside and all she wanted to be was a nurse.

Caring and considerate and compassionate, she spent her young adult years tending to the sick and the lame. White or black, rich or poor, it made no difference to his mother. She cared for them just the same.

Now, knowing what his father had done, or at least, what it appeared that he'd done, Clayton had no answers. The very thought of his father's treachery made him ill. It didn't make sense. Clay studied people and personality traits for a living and he was darn good at it. He hadn't earned the right to be known as one of the best profilers in Australia by getting it wrong.

It didn't matter how he looked at it, the thought of his father being unfaithful rebelled against everything inside him. It was inconceivable, and yet the facts were damning. Riley had been quick to point out that all the evidence was circumstantial and that was certainly the case, but it was very hard to argue with the facts, no matter how much the two of them wanted to.

With a groan of disbelief, he finished booking his plane ticket. With no direct flight to Grafton from Canberra, he'd fly to Sydney and take a connection. He'd be in Grafton later that night and would pick up a rental car from the airport. Riley had offered to collect him, but Clay had politely turned him down. While he appreciated his twin's offer, Riley, his wife and young children, lived nearly a two-hour drive away.

No, it was better that Clay fend for himself. That way, he

could come and go as he pleased and deal with whatever was necessary. Knowing there were more calls he needed to make, he dragged the phone toward him and prepared himself to break the news to his wife and to the other members of the family.

CHAPTER 6

Brandon
Sydney, New South Wales

Brandon Munro's legs pounded the pavement and his breath came fast. He swiped at the sweat that ran down his face, before the salt could burn his eyes. The December heat scorched his neck where it was exposed by his Nike T-shirt. One more mile to go and he was done.

The main street of Bondi was decorated for Christmas, reminding him the holiday was less than a week away. A smile pushed through the strain of his breathing. He couldn't wait to give Alex her gift. He'd designed it himself, with the help of a local jeweler.

The heart-shaped, sterling silver disc had been engraved with a man and a woman's hands entwined, interspersed with diamonds. He'd included an engraved message on the back. It was just the kind of simple piece that Alex loved. He was counting down the days until he could give it to her.

A light breeze blew in from the ocean, cooling his heated skin. He breathed in deeply of its salty tang and relished the relief it brought, however slight. He was on a day off from the Child Protection Unit where he worked as a Federal Police Investigator. It was a stressful, demanding job and by the end of the week, he was usually totally drained. Not that he regretted his transfer. After all, the CPU was where he'd reconnected with his wife, Alex. He smiled again at the memory. The phone in the pocket of his gym shorts rang, interrupting his thoughts. His heart stopped cold.

Oh, Christ. The baby. Was it already on its way?

Alex's due date was only three days away. It was why she'd insisted he take his phone with him when he left for his daily jog. 'It could happen at any time,' she'd said to him. Not that he needed the reminder.

Having already been through the drama of a birth when Alex had been pregnant with Bella, he thought he'd be much more casual about the imminent arrival of this baby, but the truth of it was, even the mention of his wife enduring another birth, had him almost quivering with fear.

For reasons beyond his control, he hadn't been there when his first child, Sam, had been born and even though he'd been present when his daughter arrived, the labor had been long and difficult, for both Alex and the baby. He was terrified that might happen again.

Alex's pelvis was narrow, or so the doctors had said by way of explanation the last time, and the risk that the baby might get stuck was higher than normal. An emergency C-section was always a possibility and as Alex's due date came ever nearer, the stress of the impending birth was getting to him. He'd suggested, more than a month ago, that Alex consider a planned C-section, where they could prepare themselves ahead of time. There would be no emergency, no panic, just a mom and a baby who were both safe and happy. But Alex would have none of it.

Despite the risks, she was adamant their baby would be born naturally. She'd managed it twice before; she was sure she could manage it again. Brandon wasn't so certain, but he agreed to let her have another go. It was her body, after all. He prayed he wouldn't regret it.

He slowed his steps and tugged the phone out of his shorts and then sighed in relief when he spied the Caller ID. It was Clayton, his brother. It wasn't Alex at all. The baby was right where it should be, safe and sound inside his wife's belly. The tension gripping his insides eased and he pressed the button to answer the call.

"Clayton, how are you mate? What's happening? How are Ellie and the kids?"

———

Brandon ran the last few yards and pulled up at his front gate, his breath ragged and his heart pounding. His face burned from exertion and a smoldering anger. He could have caught a cab home and the thought had crossed his mind for a second or two after he ended the call from Clayton, but his head had been spinning with shock and he'd needed the time to calm down.

Dragging in a deep breath, he forced his heart rate slower and then jogged up the steps to his house. In the early years of their marriage, he and Alex had lived in a luxury condominium overlooking Bondi Beach and although it had three bedrooms, there was no back yard to speak of. With a seven-year-old and an eighteen-month-old, the condo had outlived its usefulness. Now, with another baby due any minute, he was glad they'd made the decision to sell.

They'd bought a house not far away and had managed to retain most of their ocean view. The house was older, but beautifully renovated and boasted the biggest back yard in Bondi. They'd lived there since Bella's birth and Brandon delighted in calling it home. Now, as he crossed the wide front porch that wrapped itself around all four sides of the house, he dreaded entering his home.

Alex glanced up from her place on the couch and immediately looked alarmed. "Brandon, my goodness! What happened? You look awful! I told you it was too hot to go for a run."

He shook his head, struggling to find the words. *What could he say?* What could he tell her? Alex's Dad had died years ago. She loved Brandon's father like he was her own and the feeling had always been mutual. Now he was about to tell her the fine, upstanding, much-admired patriarch of the Munro family and pillar of the Grafton community might be dying—and even worse, that he could be a liar and a cheat.

At his continued silence, Alex's frown deepened and she struggled awkwardly to her feet. The baby bulged in front of her and he was reminded of how close the birth was. It wasn't the time to be upsetting her. Her blood pressure had been up the week before, higher than it had been all through her pregnancy and her doctor had warned her to take it easy.

Watching her, he drew in a breath and then slowly let it out. He couldn't do it to her. He couldn't take the risk. It was important she remain calm and relaxed—that's what her OB had said. Brandon sure as hell didn't want to be the one to make things happen before they were ready.

Decision made, he shook his head and turned away, determined to spare her the upset and pain his revelations would bring. Unfortunately, she was having none of it.

"Brandon Munro, stop right there and tell me what the hell is going on!"

He tensed and halted mid-stride. His legs turned to concrete. Taking another moment, he filled his lungs to capacity and eased around to face her.

"Brandon, you're scaring me. Please, tell me what's happened." She had her hand on her belly and his heart clenched in fear.

"It's... It's nothing to get worked up about, sweetheart. Please, sit back down on the couch. The doctor told you to stay calm. It's best for you and the baby."

Alex's eyes narrowed in warning. Knowing what was to follow, Brandon braced himself for her outburst.

"Don't talk to me about what's best for me and the baby. Tell me what's wrong this minute! Tell me, before I really get upset. Something has happened. I can tell from the way you look. Now, stop being silly and just give it up."

His shoulders slumped on a sigh. He should have known

he wouldn't be able to keep it from her. "Okay, okay," he muttered, "but I want you to sit back down, first."

She stared at him a moment longer and then nodded and resumed her seat, her frown of concern still firmly in place. Taking a seat beside her, he took her hand in his. She snatched it back and her hands went to cover her mouth.

"Oh, my God! It's my mother, isn't it? She's had an accident, hasn't she? I told her not to go mountain climbing at her age, but would she listen? Of course not! She thinks just because she's in her seventies, she should still be able to do what she pleases, even if it's something as foolhardy as—"

"It's not your mother. She's fine. At least, I think she is."

Alex groaned with relief. "Oh, thank goodness! You're sure?"

"Yes, I'm sure."

The frown was back between Alex's eyes. "Then who is it?"

Knowing it was better to get it over with, leaving nothing out and as unemotionally and concisely as he could, Brandon told her.

"Dammit, Alex! You're coming with me. I'm not leaving you here on your own. The baby could come any minute."

Alex bit back an impatient sigh and tried not to roll her eyes. They'd been arguing ever since Brandon told her the news. Now he was in their bedroom throwing clothes into a suitcase. She watched him with her arms crossed awkwardly over her belly and silently counted to ten.

"Brandon, be reasonable," she said, making an effort to keep her voice neutral. "If you go by car, it will take you all night to get there and that's if you drive straight through. Book a flight and don't be silly. You need to be with your family."

"You're my family, too. Or have you forgotten?"

"Of course not and I love you for wanting to stay close, but Lily's not far away. She's already on standby if the baby decides to come, and Emma and Peter are two doors down. If anything happens, I'll call them. They'll get me to the hospital on time."

Brandon shook his head, his face grim. "No. I'm not leaving you here to deal with the birth on your own. Don't you remember the last time?"

Alex closed her eyes and nodded. "Of course, I do," she said softly. "But it doesn't mean it will happen like that again. Besides, I was in labor with Bella for thirteen hours. If it does happen like that again, there'll be more than enough time for you to fly back from Grafton."

The stubborn look on Brandon's face didn't ease. Alex sighed quietly, knowing it was his fear that something might go wrong in the labor ward that had him so adamant about not leaving her behind. She didn't blame him. It must have been difficult for him to watch while she'd labored for so many hours, weak and exhausted and downright sore. She should have been pleased that he cared—and she was.

But it was important for him to be with his family and she was in no condition to fly. Grafton was at least an eight-hour drive away and who knew how much time Duncan had? Marguerite needed her children and it was important for Brandon to see his father—whether he wanted to or not. The Munro family were closer than any she'd ever encountered and Brandon would never forgive himself if his father died before he got there, despite how torn he was right now.

He was angry and hurt and bewildered. He was struggling to reconcile what he'd been told by Clayton with the father he admired and respected and loved. She knew exactly how he was feeling. She wasn't quite as quick as Clay to conclude Duncan's guilt, but no matter where the truth lay, there was nothing either of them could do about it, except pray and offer love and support to all those affected.

She walked up behind him and with difficulty, put her arms around his waist. Leaning her forehead against his back, she breathed in his familiar, comforting smell. They'd been married for more than a decade and she loved him now even more than she had then. It was up to her to make him see he needed to be with his family. He needed to be with his mother and brothers and sisters and he needed to visit his father and make peace the best way he could—before it was too late.

His shoulders slumped on a sigh. He turned around to face her and took her gently in his arms. Tilting her chin up with his fingers, he leaned down and kissed her softly, tenderly on the mouth. When he spoke, his voice was thick with emotion.

"I love you, Alex Munro. You can't imagine how much."

She reached up and cupped his cheek with her hand. "I think I can. I love you just as much."

He rested his chin on her head and breathed in the scent of her hair. They stood in silence, drawing strength from each other. It was a long while later when Brandon finally spoke.

"I have to catch a plane, don't I?"

Alex stared up at him and nodded then whispered, "Yes, you do."

CHAPTER 7

Declan
Canberra, Australian Capital Territory

The sound of Declan Munro's phone vibrating against the cherry wood coffee table snagged Chloe Munro's attention. She'd turned it to silent on purpose to avoid waking her husband. He was on his second day of nightshift at the busy Australian Federal Police Headquarters in Civic and he needed every minute of sleep he could get. He'd barely been down an hour. She was determined to let nothing, and no one, disturb him.

The phone stopped. Less than twenty seconds later, it started vibrating again. Chloe leaned over from her place on the couch and picked it up. The Caller ID read *Brandon*. She debated about answering it. Brandon was probably calling his brother to pass the time. They often caught up and it wasn't unusual to hear Declan on the phone to one of his family members three or four times a week. They were a tight-knit bunch who enjoyed keeping in close contact and sharing each other's lives. It was touching to see the effort each one of them put in, despite the large distances that separated them.

Of the seven Munro children, Declan and Clayton were the only ones who lived in Canberra. Tom and Brandon lived in Sydney, and Riley lived a good day's drive away in northern New South Wales. Josie and Chanel, the youngest of the siblings, lived interstate and shared an apartment together in Brisbane. It wasn't often the nine of them were together in one place and the rare times it happened were treasured.

Once again, the phone fell silent. Brandon wouldn't know Declan had pulled night shift. He'd no doubt leave a message and wait for his brother to call. She'd barely finished the thought when the phone rang yet again.

Three calls in as many minutes. Something was off.

Either Brandon had exciting news…

The thought no longer formed in her head and she snatched up the phone and answered. Of course he had exciting news! She couldn't believe she'd forgotten!

"Declan, thank Christ you picked up. I've been trying to get hold of you."

"Sorry, Brandon, it's Chloe. Declan's in bed asleep. So, tell me! Is it a boy or a girl? How did everything go?" Her questions were greeted with silence. A moment later, Brandon spoke.

"Chloe?"

"Yes, it's me. I noticed you calling and remembered the baby! That *is* what you're calling about, isn't it? Alex has had the baby?"

"Um…no. No, she hasn't and that's not the reason I'm calling. I…I need to speak to Declan. Is he around?"

Chloe frowned at Brandon's somber tone. "He's on nightshift tonight. He's having a sleep. Is everything all right?"

Brandon sighed heavily and Chloe's concern increased. "No, everything's not all right," he said. "In fact, everything's fu— I mean, messed up."

Chloe went cold. She couldn't imagine what had happened to fill Brandon's voice with such sadness. He was usually always so cheerful. Now, he sounded upset and distant. A sudden sense of foreboding rooted her to the spot. She opened her mouth, but the words wouldn't come. Knowing she had to ask, she forced herself to speak.

"Is it Alex? The baby? Please, tell me they're okay. Please, Brandon. I need to know."

"Alex and the baby are fine. I'm sorry if I scared you. It's not them. It's... Are you sure you can't wake Declan? It's really important I speak with him."

"He's barely been asleep an hour. He has to be at work by six. I'd rather not disturb him, if I can help it. Can I give him a message when he wakes?"

Another heavy sigh sounded in her ear. "Tell him...tell him Dad's in hospital in Grafton. He's suffered a bleed on his brain. He's...he's not doing so well."

Shock rushed through her and left her gasping. She shook her head in disbelief. "Oh, my goodness, Brandon. What happened? Is he going to be all right?"

"The doctors aren't saying much about his prognosis. He's been unconscious since he was brought in. They operated on him and stopped the bleeding, but apparently, these things can take time to develop, one way or the other. At this stage, we really don't know."

Chloe could still not believe it. "How's your mother? She must be out of her mind with worry."

Brandon gave a non committal answer and Chloe could only assume he hadn't yet spoken to her. "When are you heading up there to see him?"

"Alex has insisted I fly up tonight. She's too far along to fly with me, so she's staying put. If she goes into labor, I'll be on the next plane back."

Chloe bit her lip. "I think I need to wake Declan. This is something he needs to know. He'll want to fly up there with you, if he can. He'll want to be there for his mom."

"Yeah, I think that might be for the best. I doubt he'll want to work tonight once he's told Dad is so ill. Clayton's flying from Canberra into Sydney and will get a connection from there. Declan might be able to get on the same flight."

"I'll look into it right away. You need to be together. Your father and mother need you and you all need each other. It's times like this that family is so important. Believe me, I know."

This time, Brandon's sigh was filled with relief. "Thanks, Chloe. I appreciate your support and I'm sure the rest of the family will, too."

"Give my love to your parents and tell them I'm praying hard."

"I will. Please have Declan call me as soon as he can."

Chloe ended the call and set the phone back on the coffee table. She was loathe to wake her husband, but she didn't have a choice. His father was gravely ill, perhaps dying. *Who knew how much time he might have left?* It was important Declan be there. At the very least, he'd want to know.

She stood up from where she'd been sitting on the couch and immediately swayed with dizziness. She'd been feeling lightheaded and nauseous for the past few weeks. It would come and go in waves and appear and disappear without warning. She'd put it down to a virus her daughter must have brought home from day care. Even though Jessica hadn't displayed any symptoms herself, it was possible she'd come into contact with it and had passed it on to her mother.

Chloe grimaced. It wouldn't be the first time. At fifteen months of age, Jessie was still in the baby room at the local day care center and seemed to come into contact with more than her fair share of stomach bugs and other viruses. No doubt she'd have a sturdy immune system by the time she started formal schooling. No doubt they all would.

With the wave of dizziness passing, Chloe walked down the hall toward the bedroom she shared with her husband. She glanced in on their daughter, who'd settled for an afternoon nap not long after Declan had gone to bed. Jessie's eyes were closed and her breathing was deep and even. Chloe smiled, pleased to see her little girl was asleep. Dinner time was always so much more pleasant when she was rested.

Chloe continued further down the hall. Her gaze skimmed over the collection of framed photographs that lined either side of the dark-green walls. The twelve-foot-high, pressed-metal ceilings allowed for a veritable gallery of pictures to be hung on display at eye level and upwards. What started out as a hobby was fast becoming an obsession, particularly since the birth of Jessica. Chloe never tired of spending quiet time with her baby and capturing the endless special moments through her lens.

The majority of the pictures were family photographs. Declan came from a family of nine. She came from a family of six. In addition, there were spouses, children, nieces and nephews... She was never short of subjects.

Reaching the end of the hall, Chloe drew in a deep breath before she eased open the half-closed door that led into their bedroom. The aged, polished timber floorboards were soft and shiny beneath her bare feet. Despite his fatigue, Declan's clothes hung neatly over the back of the carved wooden rocking chair that stood in one corner of the room. He'd been a neat freak when she'd met him and three years of married life hadn't changed a thing. She supposed she was lucky. Plenty of women would envy her having a man who cleaned up after himself—especially when he did it without having to be asked.

The man in question lay spread-eagled across the king-sized bed, naked apart from his underwear. His arms were flung out above his head, his lips slightly parted in sleep. His brown hair was mussed and probably in need of a haircut. Secretly, she loved it a little longer like that. It reminded her of the wild streak in him, hidden beneath his designer suits.

Not many of his work colleagues knew how much he loved to ride his 1199 Panigale Ducati motorcycle at full throttle along the freeway north to Sydney in the middle of the night, dressed from head to toe in black leather. It was his way of relaxing and clearing his head of the daily stresses of working in the Child Protection Unit. She understood his need to indulge in something a long way removed from the often-depressing reality of his job.

The thought of waking him less than an hour after he went to bed still didn't sit well with her, but what she'd told Brandon was right. Having their father lying seriously ill in hospital was something Declan would want to know, despite his attempt to catch up on much-needed sleep.

Chloe sighed. He'd been working so hard lately, with many late nights at the office. He was in the middle of an international online pedophile investigation and they were slowly closing in. It was imperative for Declan's team of investigators to keep up the momentum and that meant long work shifts. When he did finally make it to bed, his sleep was often broken by Jessie waking in the night, cross and irritable from teething.

And now Chloe was going to interrupt his slumber yet again...

She eased herself onto the bed and laid her hand upon his cheek. He stirred and turned his head to press a kiss against her palm. Her belly somersaulted with need, as it always did when he touched her. His eyes fluttered open.

"What is it?" he murmured, his voice clouded with sleep.

"I'm sorry to wake you, darling. I-I just took a call from Brandon."

A slight frown marred the smooth skin of his forehead. "What's he calling about?"

"It's your father. He's in the hospital."

Declan half sat, coming fully awake. "In the hospital? Is he all right?"

"No, darling. I'm...I'm afraid he's not."

By the time Chloe finished telling Declan what she knew, he'd dressed and packed an overnight bag. A quick text to Clayton about his flight details and Declan managed to secure a seat on the same plane to Sydney with a connection to Grafton. He kept himself occupied with the minutiae of leaving in an emergency, including a phone call to his boss, Gary Julian, to request the time off.

Throughout his preparations, he did his best to come to terms with the news that his father was critically ill. The fact that a brain aneurysm had ruptured was frightening. That he'd been in a coma since they'd found him, even more so.

Chloe watched him make his arrangements, her expression full of sadness and concern. She'd offered to come with him, but hanging around a hospital room with a toddler was no fun for anyone. He was glad she hadn't delayed telling him, even if he desperately needed to rest. He'd been pulling unbelievably long hours at work, buried so deep within the belly of his current investigation that he barely had time to come up for air—but he needed to be with his family more. It was as simple as that.

He looked around for his phone, intent on calling his mother and spied it on the coffee table in the living room. She'd be crazy with worry for his dad. The two of them were inseparable. He couldn't imagine how she'd cope without him by her side.

Scrolling through his contacts, he found his mother's number and listened impatiently while the call dialed out. Chloe came into the room and leaned against the door frame with her arms loosely folded across her chest. He looked up at her and his heart warmed at the love and support in her gaze.

He thought of his father lying near death in the hospital and his heart went out once again to his mother. If anything ever happened to Chloe, he was certain, beyond a doubt, his life would fragment into pieces and he'd never be able to put them back together.

His mother's pre-recorded message sounded in his ear. He sighed quietly, knowing she probably had her phone on silent or even switched off in deference to the rules of the hospital. No doubt she was glued to his father's side. He felt a fleeting moment of pity for the nursing staff that might have the temerity to suggest she take a break and leave off her vigil.

He left a brief message, letting his mother know he was on his way, and then ended the call. Chloe stepped nearer and slipped her arms around his waist. He took her in his arms and leaned his chin against her hair, taking comfort from the familiar scent of her shampoo.

He missed her already.

CHAPTER 8

Marguerite

Grafton, New South Wales

From her position on the wooden bench that stood on the banks of the Clarence River where she'd escaped to after leaving her husband's side, Marguerite stared across the wide expanse of water and brushed away her tears. She still couldn't believe what had happened.

Even her years of nursing experience hadn't prepared her for the shocking sight of Duncan, usually so vibrant and full of life, lying so still and deathly pale in the ICU. It was always different when the patient was someone you loved. It had been the same when her daughter, Josie, had badly broken her leg.

The sudden departure of a pelican lifting up and over the water momentarily captured Marguerite's attention. She watched its graceful progress along the river, its wings stretched far out wide. It was joined by another one and they flew together, proud and majestic, and eventually disappeared from view.

She sighed and her troubled thoughts circled back to Duncan. She could tell that Riley was struggling to reconcile what had been found in the hotel room with the father he knew. She could understand his confusion. She was perplexed, too. In her heart, she was certain Duncan hadn't been cheating on her, but her head kept doing its best to override it.

She'd been married to him for forty years. She knew him as well as she knew herself. With every fiber of her being, she refused to believe he'd been unfaithful. And yet there was the lingerie, and the candles, the oils, the lubricant, the rose, the champagne in an ice bucket on a tray that held two glasses...

Her husband had been expecting a woman—a woman he intended to have sex with and as far as she knew, that woman wasn't her. Though she steeled herself against it, the thought of his betrayal cut deep. The last time she'd seen him, had only been that morning. He'd been in the garden, admiring the bountiful crop of roses. She'd waved at him from the kitchen window and he'd cheerfully returned her greeting. She'd even seen him snip off a large, red bud and hold it up to his nose, breathing in its heady fragrance. Now she couldn't help but wonder if it was the same rose that had been found in the hotel room.

A fresh wave of tears burned behind her eyes. She leaned forward until she was on the edge of the bench where she'd taken refuge. Resting her head in her hands, she breathed through the pain. There were facts and then there was knowledge. She *knew* her husband. He would die before he cheated on her. It was as simple as that. There had to be another explanation.

She'd given him her love and her loyalty for more than forty years and he'd reciprocated in kind. Now he was gravely ill, perhaps even dying. She'd continue to show him the loyalty he deserved until he was well enough to explain what had happened and how he'd come to find himself in such a compromising situation. They'd laugh about it and then even cry at how lucky they were that he'd pulled through and had lived to tell them about it.

Sitting upright, she brushed at the tears on her cheeks and drew in a deep breath. It did no one any good to sit around moping—least of all, Duncan. He needed her love and he needed her support. It was thought that many patients in a coma could still hear things around them, were still aware of their environment. She needed to pull herself together and get back there, to the hospital. To her husband.

CHAPTER 9

Tom

Sydney, New South Wales

Detective Sergeant Tom Munro leaned back in his chair and glanced at the clock on the far wall of the squad room. A couple of hours to go and he'd be out of there. It had been a quiet day. He and his fellow police negotiator, Andy Warwick, had filled the day completing paperwork and catching up on the humdrum of other less-important activities that got pushed aside whenever a call came in for their help.

He glanced at Andy where he sat at his desk not more than three or four feet away and noticed he was playing Solitaire on his computer.

"What are you up to for Christmas, Andy? Got any plans?"

Andy looked over at him and shrugged. "I'm not sure what Cally has planned. She's talking about going back to Watervale and spending a few days with Kate."

"That's right. I forgot she went to school with Riley's wife. How often do they catch up?"

"Not as often as they'd like. Cally's never keen to visit in case she runs into her father. They reconciled when Grace was born, but their relationship is still rather strained. She prefers to avoid him if she can. Kate and Riley came down to Sydney for Grace's baptism and they caught up then."

"Of course. I forgot about the baptism. That was only a couple of weeks ago, wasn't it? Lily and I were out of town, so we missed seeing them."

Andy grinned. "Yeah, it was a shame. We had a great day. Unfortunately, Cally couldn't change the date. I think she booked it in about a minute after Grace was born. She was determined to get our daughter christened while she could still fit into Jack's christening gown. It had been made by her Aunt Mary while Cally was still pregnant. Because Mary died when Jack was eight the gown holds enormous significance." He shrugged. "It didn't matter to me. I only want to see her happy."

Tom nodded, his expression thoughtful. "She's been good for you, mate. It wasn't even a year ago that your life was more than a struggle. Now it seems like you can't keep the smile off your face."

"Yeah, you're right about that," Andy said. "I can barely remember the dark days before I met her and yet I'd lived more than two decades with the ghosts of my childhood." A fierce glint entered his gaze. "I swear to God my kids will never know a day of unhappiness. Not if I can help it."

Tom's face filled with understanding. "How are they?"

Andy chuckled. "Jack's turning eleven this January and is smart and cheeky and fun. Gracie's already six weeks old. Time sure gets away, doesn't it?"

"Yes, it does. It seems like only yesterday Lily and I were bringing our kids home from the hospital, but Cassie's going on for sixteen and Joe's just become a teenager. You wait until you have teens in the house, Andy. You'll be pulling your hair out."

Andy grinned and Tom could tell he thought Tom was exaggerating. He grimaced and bit his lip. *If only...*

The shrill peal of the phone on his desk interrupted his unsettled thoughts. He reached across and answered it. "Tom Munro."

"Tom, thank Christ I got hold of you. I've been trying to call you for the past hour."

"Really? What's up, Declan?"

"I take it you haven't heard?"

"Heard what?"

The silence on the other end of the phone was long enough to give Tom pause. He straightened in his chair. "Declan? What's going on?"

"It's Dad. He's not good. He's in hospital in Grafton. From what I've been told, at the moment, it's touch and go."

"Shit. What happened?"

Declan recounted what he knew and Tom shook his head back and forth in shock and disbelief. "Christ. How's Mom taking it? Have you spoken to her?"

"No, I tried to call her a little while ago, but I only got her voicemail. She probably has her phone switched off."

"Does everyone else know?"

"I'm not sure. Brandon called me and Clayton told him. I'm assuming Riley was the one who called Clay, given that Riley's living the closest to Mom and Dad. Clay said Riley's been at the hospital all afternoon."

Tom ran a hand over his face and grimaced, trying to sort through his tangle of thoughts. Right now, Lily was at home with Cassie and Joe, but she was supposed to be attending her best friend's bridal shower later that evening. As the matron of honor, it was important that she be there. She intended to leave for the party as soon as Tom arrived home.

Cassie was expecting him to drive her up to Avalon, where she was staying with a handful of her girlfriends. They'd arranged to have an end-of-year send off for a couple of girls who were leaving high school. She'd been nagging him about it for more than a week, insisting he be home in plenty of time. And then there was Joe's end-of-year school play.

For once, he'd been given the lead role and he couldn't wait for his family to witness his prowess on the stage. It was all he'd talked about for nearly a month. The play was set for tomorrow night. Tom had promised his son he'd be there. He'd arranged to have the time off, but if he had to be in Grafton...

Then there was that doctor's appointment the day after that; the one he kept putting off. Not to mention the pile of invitations to Christmas parties both he and Lily had accepted. One of them was his office party.

Knowing Christmas was less than a week away sent a surge of anxiety rushing through him. *What if his father were still in hospital at Christmas?* It would be downright shitty for all of them to have to celebrate the day with the knowledge that their much-loved patriarch was lying sick in the ICU. The very thought was beyond depressing.

He clutched at his hair and groaned. There was nothing for it. He had to go. He had to be there for his mother and his father—not to mention his brothers and sisters. He was the oldest in the family. He had no choice. It was during times like this, times of family crises, when he felt the weight of their expectations the most—and he'd never let them down.

The memory of his mother's brush with breast cancer a few years earlier flashed through his mind. His father had been a mess, unable to bear the sight of his wife, gaunt and pale, vomiting and in pain, as the deadly dose of chemicals poured into her veins in an effort to kill the tumor that had taken up residence in her chest. The family had turned to Tom, their oldest brother, to take the lead and show them the way out of the pain and shock and numbness of knowing the treatment might not work. He'd risen to the occasion without hesitation. That was why he would walk away from all of his daily obligations, his commitments, all the ties he had to normal life and go to them.

"Tom? Hey, Tom? Are you all right?"

Tom blinked and shook his head, becoming aware of the increasing urgency in Andy's voice. He looked across at his friend and work colleague and attempted a strained smile.

"I-I don't know. I don't think so. M-my father's been rushed to hospital. He's in the ICU. They're not sure if he's going to live."

"Oh, mate, that's bloody awful. You have to get out of here. You have to go and see him. Where does he live?"

"Grafton."

"At least you can get a direct flight from Sydney. What can I do to help?"

"Thanks, Andy. I appreciate your offer. I-I'm not sure if there's anything you can do. *I'm* not even sure what to do."

"Call Lily. That's what you need to do."

Tom nodded. "You're right. I need to call Lily. She'll know what to do."

CHAPTER 10

Josie and Chanel
Brisbane, Queensland

Marguerite had almost made it back to the hospital when her cell phone rang. She hadn't been able to bring herself to listen to the countless messages that had been left during the time since she'd been in the ICU. No doubt Riley had called his brothers and sisters. Even now, they were more than likely making plans to come and see their father and to be with her and offer their comfort.

Not that she begrudged them their actions. She loved that they cared enough to come. She just didn't know how she was going to face them, knowing what they knew. They thought their father hung the moon and the stars. It had always been that way. Now, some of them were probably questioning their faith in the man they called Dad. The very thought that their loyalties might be tested filled her with sadness. They didn't know him like she did. They didn't know it couldn't possibly be true. All she could do was try and convince them to ignore what the evidence implied and trust her and her unshakable belief in their father.

She sighed. It wasn't going to be easy. All five of her sons were in law enforcement. They'd been trained to look at the evidence and draw logical conclusions from it. They'd struggle more than her daughters with what had happened.

Tugging her phone out of her handbag, she checked the Caller ID and her heart clenched.

Chanel. Of all her children, her youngest would be affected the least by the evidence at the scene. She'd grown up as Duncan's little girl. There was nothing anyone could say or do to make her think badly of the man she still called Daddy. Marguerite was grateful for her daughter's fierce loyalty. She was going to need her support.

Drawing in a deep breath, she answered the call. "Hi, sweetheart. How are you?"

"Mom, how's it going? I have you on speakerphone. Josie's here, too. She's just come home from work."

"Hi, Mom. I'm waving from the other side of the room."

Marguerite heard the laughter in Josie's greeting and bit her lip against the surge of emotion that threatened to undo her. From the light-hearted tone in her daughters' voices, it was clear neither of them knew. She drew in a breath and did her best to sound normal. "H-hi, girls. It's... It's good to hear from you."

"What's wrong, Mom? You sound...funny," Chanel asked.

"N-nothing. I mean..." Her spurt of bravado dissolved. The last few hours had caught up with her. Fresh tears burned behind her eyes and emotion clogged her throat.

"What is it, Mom? What's happened?" asked Josie, her tone quickly sobering.

With faltering breaths and broken sentences, Marguerite choked out the news as best she could. While she made mention of the hotel room and the fact he may have been expecting a woman, she spared them all but the barest of details. When at last she was finished, she was met with shocked silence.

"How could he?" cried Josie.

"I won't believe it!" shouted Chanel.

The girls spoke over the top of each other, getting increasingly louder in their protestations and denials until Marguerite was forced to hold the phone away from her ear. She understood how they felt. She was still reeling from the news and she'd had a few hours to get used to it. At last, they seemed to realize she was no longer responding and fell silent.

"Mom, are you okay?" Josie asked, her voice low and shaky.

"Yes, sweetheart. I'm okay. I'm fine. I-I guess I'm in shock a little, too, like you, but I'm fine. It's your father I'm worried about."

"I'm on my way, Mom. I don't know about Josie, but I'm driving down there as soon as I can throw a few things in my bag."

"I-I'll call my office and explain that Dad's sick," Josie added quickly. "I'm sure they'll let me take some time off. I'll come down with Chanel. We can share the driving."

A surge of relief flooded through Marguerite. As much as she'd dreaded her children's reactions, she couldn't deny she was thankful they would be with her soon. Right now, she needed her family around her. She needed to draw strength from their numbers, from their support and from their unconditional love.

"Okay, darlings. Please, drive safely. I'll see you soon."

With a chorus of solemn good-byes, the girls ended the call. Marguerite sighed. It would take them three or four hours to drive down from Brisbane, depending upon how often they stopped for rest breaks. She expected to see them later that evening. As soon as she'd visited with Duncan again, she'd go home and make up the beds in at least a couple of the spare rooms. It was likely her daughters would stay with her. They normally did.

It was possible the boys would stay there, too. With Riley a two-hour drive away, it would be more convenient for her sons to stay with her, at the family home and of course, there was plenty of room. She and Duncan still lived in the home they'd had since they were married. With the birth of each child, another room had been added and it had undergone renovations over the years, but the bones of the house were as original and solid as the day they'd purchased it.

She remembered that day like it was yesterday. Duncan

had been so excited to show her. He'd found it by accident when he was driving on the outskirts of Grafton only a month before their wedding. It had been a rush, but the sale had gone through the day before their marriage and he'd worn a smile as wide as the Clarence River the evening he'd carried her over the threshold as his wife. The house held so many memories and most of them happy. Now...

She didn't even want to complete the thought. With a concerted effort, she pushed the circumstances surrounding Duncan's medical emergency into the furthest reaches of her mind and strode through the doorway of the hospital. Her husband was gravely ill and he needed her. Nothing else mattered.

CHAPTER 11

Clayton
Mascot Airport, Sydney

Clayton stared out through the glass walls of the airport and into the coming night. The lights of the city glowed softly in the distance. He pulled his carry-on suitcase behind him and headed toward the gate where the plane to Grafton was due to depart. Brandon, Tom and Declan were presumably already there, waiting for him. He and Declan had planned to travel together from Canberra, but it hadn't worked out that way.

As if the day hadn't been bad enough, Clayton's cab had been involved in an accident and he ended up missing his flight. He'd been lucky to escape injury and had been luckier still when he managed to score a seat on the last plane of the day. It was fortunate he could still make his connection.

His thoughts turned to Ellie and he uttered a soft sigh. At least she hadn't argued with his need to go—to be there with his family. Lately, it seemed all they did was argue and he knew the reason why. It had nothing to do with the way they felt about each other or even about his parents. He'd love Ellie until his dying breath and he knew she felt the same. What was causing the friction between them was his daughter.

Olivia had been a little over four when he'd married Ellie. His daughter couldn't possibly have any memories of her mother, having only been a baby when her mother had died, but still, the child clung to the idea of her and stubbornly refused to open her heart to her father's new wife. He and Ellie had been married for more than six years, but Olivia continued in her refusal to recognize Ellie as the woman who had been more of a mother to her than the one who'd given her life.

Clayton was caught in the middle and didn't have a clue what to do or how to go about fixing it. He was a well-known and highly respected police profiler. He looked into the psyche of people for a living and determined what made them tick, but it was different when it was his family under the microscope.

He spied the back of Declan's dark blond head and then recognized his other two brothers. Brandon and Tom held large takeaway coffee cups in their hands. All three of them looked grim. He closed the distance between them and greeted each of them with a brief hug.

"Hey, Clay. Good to see you," Declan murmured.

"You're looking good, bro," Tom said.

"You finally made it," Brandon muttered.

"Yeah," Clayton replied. "No thanks to the cabbie."

"It's lucky you weren't hurt," Tom said, eyeing him closely.

"Yeah, that's just what Mom would need. Another family member in hospital," Brandon added.

The reminder of why they had gathered sobered all of them. Gazes dropped to their feet and coffee cups were tilted toward suddenly silent lips. Clayton scuffed the toe of his boot across the shiny surface of the airport floor. A moment later, he cleared his throat. "It couldn't have happened at a worst time."

"Is there ever a good time for something like this?" Brandon asked. "It's not like Dad asked for his blood vessel to rupture."

"I think Clay's referring to the fact Christmas is right

around the corner, Brandon," Tom said, shooting Brandon a warning look to calm down.

"I'm with Clay," Declan added. "We all know how much Dad loves to celebrate the holidays. He's going to be pissed if he sleeps through it."

"Don't worry, he'll pull through. He's as tough as a piece of leather. I'm sure this won't do him in," Tom added.

A renewed surge of anger rushed through Clayton's veins. "And then what? Is Mom supposed to simply forgive and forget and welcome him back with open arms?"

His outburst was met by frowns of confusion from Tom and Declan. Brandon jammed his hands into his pockets and lowered his gaze.

"What the hell are you talking about?" Tom asked.

"What would Mom have to forgive? Like Brandon said, Dad didn't ask for this to happen," Declan added.

Clayton looked from one brother to the other. The confusion remained on their faces. He shook his head and frowned darkly at Brandon before eyeing his other brothers. "Don't tell me you don't know? Didn't Brandon tell you?"

Clayton and the other two turned as one to face the brother in question. Brandon stared at the floor, an uncomfortable expression on his face.

"I was the one who called Tom. He only knows what I do. So, what didn't you tell me, Brandon?" Declan asked, his voice low and threatening.

"For Christ's sake, Bran, what the hell is Clayton talking about?" growled Tom.

Brandon's cheeks reddened under the combination of their stares. "I didn't mean to keep it from you, Dec. It's just that, when I called with the news, you were asleep and Chloe answered your phone. I-I didn't want to just blurt it out to her. Then later, we sorted out the flight details through texts. I-I didn't want to text you about it. I wanted to call you back and tell you, but I didn't know what to say. I still don't know."

Tom turned to Clayton. "So, we're back to you. What the hell's happened to get you all riled up about Dad?"

Clayton stared at him and then shook his head, trying to find the words. He threw a glance in Brandon's direction, hoping his brother might help him out, but once again, Brandon avoided his eye. Drawing in a deep breath, he prayed for the right words. With a concerted effort, he kept his anger in check and as quickly and concisely as he could, told them everything.

After filling in the necessary paperwork, Clayton collected the keys to the rental car from the man behind the counter outside the Grafton airport and went and joined his brothers who were waiting nearby with their luggage.

"Right, whoever wants a ride, feel free to join me. Anyone who would rather sort out their own transport, be my guest. Riley texted me to say he left the hospital an hour ago. He had to go. Kate and the twins are sick with the flu. He's needed at home. But he did say there's been no change with Dad. He's still in a coma. No better. No worse."

Brandon and Tom sidled away. They'd been giving him the cold shoulder the entire flight—ever since he'd told Tom and Declan about their father's philandering. He didn't get it. *How could they defend the man?* Riley might have urged him to keep an open mind, but Clay knew his twin was merely going through the motions. He believed what Clay believed: the evidence didn't lie. Their father was having an affair and nothing anybody said could change it.

Brandon and Tom had tried to argue that nobody knew for sure, that what Joel Parker had found could have been misconstrued, but they were a family of police officers. Law enforcement ran through their blood. They couldn't honestly believe there was any other explanation. It was what had kept his anger simmering since the very moment he heard.

"I'll get my own car," Brandon muttered. "It'll be easier if we have two." He moved off toward the rental car counter.

"I-I might go with him, keep him company," Tom added hurriedly, avoiding Clayton's gaze.

Clayton stemmed his irritation and offered a curt nod. "What about you, Dec? Are you going to travel with me?" |

Declan nodded, his face closed. "Yeah, I'll ride with you."

"Good." He glanced at Tom. "We'll see you at the hospital."

Twenty minutes later, Clayton and Declan met Tom and Brandon in the car park outside the Emergency Room, the latter having only just arrived.

"We've just come from the ICU," Clayton said by way of greeting. "It's past visiting hours and the staff won't let us in." He grimaced. "They're restricting Dad's visitors to one at a time and they say he's had enough for today. Uncle Gary and Aunt Susie dropped by and Mom and Riley were here most of the afternoon. The nurse also confirmed what Riley told us a little while ago: Dad's condition remains unchanged, which apparently, is a good sign."

Brandon frowned. "So that's it? We've flown all the way up here on the first available flight and we can't even see him?"

Clayton stared at him with narrowed eyes. "Not tonight, anyway."

Brandon's eyes glinted with anger in the well-lit car park. "That's bullshit. They can't refuse to allow us to see him. He's our father."

Tom put a hand on Brandon's arm in an effort to calm him down. "I think they can, mate, and what Clay says is right. If he's stable, that's a good sign. I'm sure if the staff thought there was a chance he might..."

"Die," Declan supplied.

"Yeah...die," Tom continued. "Then they'd bend the rules and let us in."

Brandon's shoulders slumped on a sigh. "You're right. I guess it means we'll see him in the morning." He looked around at the three of them. "Where are you all staying?"

CHAPTER 12

Marguerite
Grafton, New South Wales

The knock on the front door broke into Marguerite's troubled thoughts and she quickly finished hanging fresh towels on the rail in the guest bathroom. With the aid of the myriad of fairy lights Duncan had strung up across the front porch a couple of weeks ago and the life-sized Santa that glowed in the dark, a glance out the window showed the silhouettes of her sons. Her heart tripped over: They'd come.

Hurrying down the stairs, she patted her hair and smoothed out the light cotton dress she'd donned after she'd showered upon her return from the hospital. Switching on the porch light, she swung the door open wide.

"Mom!" She was enveloped in one hug after another from a quartet of large men: Her sons. Not one of them less than six feet. All of them broad-shouldered and lean, like their father.

Brandon and Tom stood off to one side and seemed to be avoiding glancing at their brothers. Clayton and Declan looked equally determined to avoid looking at their brothers. She sighed inwardly and blinked back tears, for once at a loss to help them. Each of them would need to deal with what had happened in their own way. All she could do was to love them and pray any fallout wouldn't last long.

"Boys, I'm so pleased to see you and I'm glad you chose to stay here. Come in, come in! It's been far too long since I've seen you all." She led them into the kitchen, which had always been the heart of the house. They dropped boots and light jackets and suitcases in the hall and followed her into the room.

The air conditioner hummed quietly on the wall, keeping the room temperature comfortably cool. The sun had set hours before, but the summer heat lingered in the air. There was often a breeze from the river that helped keep the humidity down, but tonight not even a leaf stirred in the still evening.

Her sons crowded around the kitchen counter and suddenly filled the room. She wasn't used to having so many men in her kitchen. It had been much too long since they'd all been there together. She frowned and tried to think back to when it had been and decided it was more than a year ago, when Riley's twins had been christened.

Busying herself at the sink, she filled the electric jug and set it on to boil, trying her best to keep her thoughts from straying to the reason they'd gathered *en masse*. She should have known it was an exercise in futility. Not more than a minute later, Clayton broached the subject.

"We went to the hospital on our way from the airport, but the nursing staff wouldn't let us in. They said visiting hours were over and that Dad was resting peacefully. Riley was there until a little over an hour before we arrived. He told us nothing's changed."

Marguerite nodded. "Yes, I left about the same time. I guess that's good news. At least he hasn't deteriorated. We can only hope and pray for the best."

She hoped she sounded more positive than she felt. For the sake of her children, she would put on a brave face and do what was required to survive this. There would be time enough in the future, after Duncan was well, to ask the questions that burned inside her.

Because, of course, he would recover. She refused to consider any other possibility. Duncan was a fighter—strong and determined and stubborn. He wouldn't die without giving his side of the story. He wouldn't dare; and she was more than prepared to listen. They'd been together for most of their lives. Whether or not he'd cheated—and she still refused to believe that he had—he deserved a fair hearing. It was the least she could do, despite the obvious opinions of some of her children.

Even now, Declan was shaking his head. "I still can't believe it, Mom. What he did to you! I want to yell and curse at him. I want to shake him and insist upon an explanation."

Clayton nodded, his expression grim. "He has some explaining to do, all right," he growled. "The minute he wakes up, I'm going to demand to know what the hell he was thinking! He'll be lucky if I don't knock him back out."

Marguerite's heart filled with sadness. She hated to see her children like this. She hated it even more that their father wasn't present to defend himself and to set things right. She only hoped that when he came out of the coma, he could.

"Declan, Clayton. Please don't speak like that. I know what Joel saw, or at least, what he says he saw, but I also know your father. I've been married to him since I was twenty-five. I don't believe he was having an affair. I don't believe it for an instant."

"Exactly," Brandon said. "It's like I've been telling you guys. We all know Dad. There's no way he'd be involved in something so...deceitful. I'll admit, when Clayton first told me, I was shocked But the more I thought about it, the more it had to be some kind of misunderstanding. Come on, guys. Dad's the most honest, upstanding, *trustworthy* man we know. His integrity and loyalty have always been beyond reproach. That's one of the reasons why we admire and love him—just like he loves us. There's no way he'd cheat on Mom. There must be some other explanation."

"Yeah, like what?" Clayton muttered, his expression revealing that he remained unconvinced. "We're all coppers. The facts are the facts. If we weren't talking about

Dad, none of you would think twice about the evidence. Okay, so it's circumstantial, but any copper worth his salt's going to—"

"But this *is* Dad," Brandon interrupted, "and Mom's right. We need to give him the benefit of the doubt. We owe him that much, surely? Right, Tom?"

All eyes turned to Tom, including Marguerite's. Tom squirmed under the combined weight of their stares and she immediately felt sorry for her oldest son.

"It's all right, Tom," she hurried to reassure him. "I know exactly how you feel. Like Brandon, when I first heard, I nearly collapsed with shock, even while my heart told me it couldn't possibly be true."

"Tom's going Switzerland on us," Brandon half joked. Marguerite frowned in confusion.

"I'm staying neutral, Mom," Tom explained. "It's the only way I can deal with it. I know all about the evidence in the hotel room, but I also know Dad. I don't want to believe he would do something like this."

Marguerite stepped forward and reached up and gave him a hug. "It's okay, Tom. We'll get through this. One way or another, we'll get through this and we'll come out the other side, I promise you."

She stood back. Her gaze encompassed the four sons who stood before her. "I mean that for all of you. We need to pull together and help each other through this and we need to help your Dad. He's gravely ill and he'll need all the love and support from us that he can get. Does everyone understand?"

She was met with varying degrees of mumbled words of assent and the tension in the room dissipated. The jug clicked off to indicate it had boiled and gave her an excuse to change the subject. She forced a smile.

"Right, who's for coffee?"

————————

An hour and a half later, after serving coffee and a light supper of sandwiches and crackers and cheese, Marguerite and her sons filed into the living room. The men threw themselves down onto the modular leather couch, while she took the matching armchair. Someone had switched the television on and for the moment, conversation between them was muted.

A knock at the door snagged her attention and her shoulders slumped in relief: *the girls.* The timing was about right. She got to her feet and opened the door and was immediately enveloped in a hug.

"Hi, Mom. We made it. It's so good to see you," Chanel said quietly, her voice subdued. Josie also greeted her with a long hug and a kiss.

"I'm so glad you arrived safely," Marguerite said, and meant it. The freeway between Grafton and Brisbane was busy any time, day or night and accidents were all too common. She worried for her youngest children. She prayed every night they'd each find their special someone to watch over them and love and protect them the way they deserved.

Josie was twenty-eight and Chanel had already turned twenty-five. Both of them were more than old enough to be looking for a life partner. Unfortunately, neither of them seemed interested. She swallowed a quiet sigh.

"Who owns the vehicles out in the drive?" Josie asked, glancing over her shoulder toward the parked cars.

"Your brothers arrived a little earlier. They've flown in from Canberra and Sydney and hired a couple of rental cars at the airport."

"They're here?" Chanel asked, her voice lifting. "All of them?"

"Yes. Riley had to go home to Watervale, but the others are inside."

"I can't remember the last time we were all together," Josie added quietly. "It must have been..." She frowned and followed her mother into the entryway.

"I was thinking the same thing a little while ago. I think it was at Rosie and Daisy's christening."

Josie nodded. "Yes, Mom, you're right. I can't believe it's been that long. We all need to make more of an effort to get together. We shouldn't wait until something like this..." Her voice faded away.

Marguerite stopped and turned to face her. "You're right, sweetheart. We shouldn't. Now, let's try and forget what's brought us all together and simply enjoy the moment for what it is. Dad wouldn't want us upset over him."

Chanel came up beside Josie, her expression serious. Tears glinted in her eyes. "How is he, Mom? Has there been any change?"

Marguerite brought the girls up to date on her way into the living room. There was an immediate chorus of subdued greetings and loving hugs and kisses as the siblings caught up with one another. They'd always been close and it warmed her heart to know that even a serious family emergency couldn't weaken the bond of love between them. She hoped, a little desperately, that it would remain that way.

CHAPTER 13

Riley
Watervale, New South Wales

After spending half the night talking things over with Kate and then the other half tossing and turning, Riley awoke to a blinding headache and the sound of the twins fighting. He groaned and buried his head under the pillow, but neither the headache nor the fighting abated.

He heard Kate in the shower and groaned again, knowing it was up to him to referee yet another disagreement between his girls. *What was it with them, anyway?* They were twins, for Christ's sake. They were supposed to read each other like a sixth sense, not fight over every minor detail. He and Clayton had been thick as thieves when they were children and they weren't even identical. What was with his daughters that made them so different?

With a deep breath, he threw on his boxers and a T-shirt and went out into the living room. He spied Daisy at the kitchen table with butter smeared all over her face; Rosie was pointing at her sister and laughing uproariously.

"Girls, what do you think you're doing? It's barely seven in the morning. And Daisy, how did you manage to get that out of the fridge?"

Daisy offered him an angelic smile and turned to point at

Rosie. Riley suppressed a groan. He should have known. His oldest daughter was always the one up to mischief. She reminded him so much of himself some days, it was downright scary.

Kate strode into the room, looking as fresh and beautiful as always. Riley didn't know how she managed it. Not only did she have twins not long out of diapers, she also had a busy art gallery to run. He often shook his head at his wife in amazement. Nothing seemed to faze her and she always had time for everyone, even him. He still couldn't believe he'd found her.

Drawing her close, he kissed her on the mouth and held her, relishing the feel of her soft body against his. She relaxed against him for a moment and then gently pulled away.

"Rosie, what have I told you about getting into the fridge? Your sister's going to have to have a bath before breakfast." Kate *tut tutted* and lifted Daisy into her arms, careful to hold her away from her dress to avoid getting soiled by the butter. Rosie looked completely unapologetic and offered nothing more than a sheepish smile by way of response. Even Riley had to grin.

The little minx. She knew exactly what she was doing. She was going to be a whole truckload of trouble for some poor guy one day. Not that Riley wanted her to grow up. Just the thought of his daughters kissing boys and doing all the things he did as a teenager nearly caused him to break out in hives. He shuddered to think how he was going to cope and was thankful it was still a long way off. Perhaps he'd get used to the idea in another decade or three.

The night before, he'd called the station in Watervale and arranged for his second-in-charge to take over for the next few days, until he knew what was happening with his father. Detective Sergeant Chase Barrington was a loyal and trustworthy officer who Riley could rely on to keep things in shape until he got back.

With a quiet sigh, he went into the kitchen and sorted out breakfast for the girls: cereal with milk and yoghurt for Rosie and toast with butter and jelly for Daisy. It was the same every morning. The girls were nothing, if not predictable. For Kate, he boiled two eggs and tossed a couple of extra pieces of bread in the toaster. She walked back in with a twin on each hip, just as he was serving.

Daisy, freshly washed and clothed, grinned and reached up to him with chubby arms and a wide, toothy smile. His heart melted. He took her from Kate's arms and threw the little girl up into the air, chuckling when she screamed and giggled in delight.

"Me, too! Me, too!" Rosie pleaded, squirming out of her mother's arms. Riley lowered Daisy to the floor and reached for her twin. After tossing her three times and with her still begging for more, Riley shook his head and stood her on the floor.

"No more. Daddy's got to go. Grandad Munro's a little sick, remember? Daddy has to visit him in hospital."

"Can we come?" Daisy asked.

"No, honey. Not yet, anyway. He's in the hospital in Grafton and I'll probably be gone most of the day. You both need to go to preschool and learn how to be good little girls."

"But, Daddy, we already are good little girls," Rosie protested, a tiny frown creasing her forehead.

Riley laughed and ruffled her hair, as straight and blond as her mother's. Daisy's was slightly darker and curled a little at the ends, but apart from the difference in hair color, most people couldn't tell them apart. He knelt down until he was at eye level with the pair of them.

"You're right, of course. You *are* good little girls. Except when you're painting your sister in butter," he mock-frowned at Rosie before turning his gaze on her twin. "With you encouraging her all the way."

The little girls laughed and giggled and looked from him to their mother and back. His heart filled with love for his family. There was nothing he wouldn't do for them.

He stood with a quiet sigh and moved over to his wife. She was dipping her toast into her egg and a little yolk had dripped onto her chin. He swiped at it tenderly with his finger and then licked it off. She followed the movement with her eyes and he noticed the way they zeroed in on his mouth.

Desire surged through him and centered in his groin, despite the headache that still persisted. He glanced at the clock on the wall of the kitchen and cursed softly under his breath. He wanted to be at the hospital when visiting hours started. It meant he had to leave now. Swallowing another sigh, he pressed a kiss to Kate's cheek and bid her farewell.

"Drive safely," she called on his way out of the room, "and say hello to your dad."

———————

Riley stared at the hospital and willed himself to walk the short distance inside. He didn't know what was keeping him immobile; it wasn't as if he hadn't been there the day before.

With an impatient shake of his head, he climbed out of his SUV and headed toward the front entrance. Kate had encouraged him to give his father the benefit of the doubt and to keep an open mind. She was right. *Prima facie*, things didn't look good, but Riley was prepared to hear his dad out before he made a decision on his guilt. He only hoped his father would have the opportunity to speak.

After riding the elevator to the third floor, he made his way down the corridor and came to a halt outside the closed double doors which led to the ICU. He half-expected his brothers to be there—or at least Clayton. His twin had told him yesterday he'd catch the next available flight. But the waiting area outside the ICU was empty. Riley drew in a deep breath before pressing the buzzer to request admittance.

The nurse who answered, agreed to let him in and a moment later, the doors swung inward. Riley followed the same route he'd taken the day before and in quick time, was once again at his father's bedside. Another nurse materialized and offered him a quiet greeting.

"He's had a restful night and everything's remained stable," she informed him. "The doctor was in to check on him only a little while ago. The bleeding has stopped, which is a good sign and the hole in the artery has begun to repair itself. Once the swelling goes down, the doctor's very hopeful your father will regain consciousness."

Riley breathed a sigh of relief and drew a chair up to the bed. His father remained just as silent and motionless as he had been the day before. The machines did their beeping and their pumping and their breathing, working hard to keep him alive.

Reaching for his father's hand, Riley clasped it tightly for a moment. "Hi, Dad. It's Riley."

There was no response. Slowly, he released it and with it, his tension and anger faded. *What was the use in maintaining a rage against a man who couldn't fight back?*

Kate was right. He needed to wait until his father was awake again and well enough to answer the questions that continued to burn in Riley's brain. He refused to contemplate what he might do if the facts he'd deliberately decided to push to one side turned out to be true...

CHAPTER 14

Clayton
Grafton Base Hospital

Clayton strode along the ground floor of the hospital and headed toward the elevators. Anger and fear simmered inside him. He barely noticed the Christmas tree in one corner of the foyer or the bright decorations on the windows. It was a little after ten and the girl manning the information desk in the lobby had assured him visiting hours had commenced.

"Would you hold up for a second, Clay? I'm sure another few minutes is hardly going to make a difference," Brandon complained from behind him, almost jogging to keep up.

Clay flicked a glance over his shoulder, but didn't break stride. "I need to see him. I need to talk to him. I need to know why he did it."

Brandon slowed and fell further behind. Clayton glanced back again and was annoyed to find his brother had come to a halt.

"For Christ's sake, would you hurry up, Brandon? What the hell are you doing?" he growled.

Brandon looked at him. "Clay, whether you break speed records getting there isn't going to make any difference at the moment. From all accounts, Dad's still in a coma."

The anger that had been lying dormant in Clay's gut

stirred to life at his brother's words and then ignited when Brandon shot him a look full of pity and slowly shook his head.

"Let it go, Clay, before it eats you up inside. We don't know what the hell happened in that hotel room, or what was about to happen. We owe it to Dad to let him explain."

In three long strides, Clayton closed the distance between them. It was all he could do not to seize his brother by the shirt and shake him. *Couldn't he see?* Brandon was a cop, like the rest of them. It was clear to anyone who bothered to read the police report what had happened—or had been supposed to happen—if his father's aneurysm hadn't burst. Saved by a ruptured blood vessel. *Whoopee do.*

Clayton clenched his fists and breathed hard in an effort to get his temper back under control. Brandon eyeballed him, almost daring him to hit him. He was every bit as tall as Clay and probably even a little more fit. His brother looked like he still worked out every day.

"Who says we owe him anything?" Clay hissed.

Brandon stared at him. "Think for a moment, for Christ's sake. According to the investigating officer, no one else entered the room. Do you know what I'm saying? The mystery woman, whoever she was, didn't show. We don't even know if she exists. Everything we've been told is circumstantial."

Brandon drew in a deep breath and sighed, forcing a more even tone. "You were raised with the same principles as I was, Clay. Innocent until proven guilty, remember? It's a tenet of our legal system we fight to uphold and one we're rightly proud of. Surely, it's the least Dad deserves? He's given his life to that very system, as have the rest of us."

Clayton's gaze narrowed. "When did you speak with Joel Parker?"

Brandon held his gaze. "Riley called me about an hour ago. He was on his way here from Watervale. He spoke to Joel this morning."

The hard expression in Clayton's eyes didn't falter. "Why didn't Riley call me?"

Brandon shrugged. Clay fumed, disappointed that his twin had rung Brandon instead of him. Brandon eyed him in silence and then cursed softly under his breath.

"You go on ahead, Clay," he muttered. "Go and see Dad. Do what you need to do. I'll catch up with you later."

"How are you getting back to Mom's?"

Brandon shrugged. "I'll work something out."

"Aren't you coming up to see him?"

"Of course, but you can go in first. Mom said they've been restricting his visitors." Brandon returned Clay's hard stare. "You need to see him more than I do."

Clay stared at him a moment longer and then spun on his heel and continued toward the elevators. He unclenched his fists and forced air deep into his lungs in an effort to calm himself down. It wasn't like he could storm into the ICU and demand answers from a man in a coma. He'd be thrown right out on his ear. Besides, it wouldn't do his father any good to upset him. For all of his anger and feelings of betrayal, Clay didn't want to harm his father's chances of recovery.

The elevator *dinged* when it reached the floor and the doors slid open with a swish. Clay went to leave and almost collided with Riley who'd been about to step inside.

"Clay! You're here. It's good to see you." Riley gave him a brief hug. "When did you get in?"

Clayton forced a half-hearted smile of acknowledgement that felt more like a grimace. "Last night. I flew to Sydney and then hopped a plane up here with Tom and Declan and Brandon. But I assume you already got all that from Brandon."

Riley's gaze narrowed at his brother's truculent tone. "What the hell's that supposed to mean? Why are you so god-damned prickly? We're all suffering here. You're not the only one. This is about Dad, not you."

Clay lowered his gaze and fought off the stab of guilt. He *was* behaving badly. Riley was right. This wasn't about him.

The fact that his twin had shared information with one of his brothers before he shared it with him shouldn't have hurt like it did.

Clay didn't realize how fragile he was, perhaps because of the ongoing battle between Ellie and Olivia. It had worn him down and shortened his temper without him being consciously aware of it. Something had to be done about it. He just didn't know what. What he did know was that now wasn't the time to deal with it.

He sighed heavily and offered Riley an apology. "I'm sorry, Riles. I'm being a prick. We're all worried about Dad and trying to come to terms with what was discovered in that hotel room… I'm struggling, mate. I really am."

Riley's lips tightened, but he nodded in understanding. "I take it you haven't seen him yet?"

"No. We came straight here from the airport last night, but they told us visiting hours were over."

"Yeah, they're keeping a pretty tight rein on his visitors at the moment. They don't want to tire him out."

"He's still unconscious?"

"Yeah, but apparently he's responding to external stimuli. If he's reacting, then he might be listening and comprehending, even if it doesn't seem like it." Riley shrugged. "They want him to put his energies into getting better."

"That's got to be a good sign, though?"

"Yeah, I think so. The nurse told me he'd had a good night."

"You must have left home early this morning? It's the best part of two hours from Watervale."

"Yeah, I left just before eight. I-I wanted to see him again."

Clayton nodded grimly. "So do I."

Riley searched Clay's face, his expression somber. "Go easy on him, Clay. We don't know anything for sure. And we don't want to slow his progress by upsetting him."

Clayton averted his gaze. "Yeah." It was all he could manage.

———————

Clay stared at the pasty, old man who lay sick and defenseless in the steel-framed hospital bed and tried to reconcile what he saw with the man he remembered. He hadn't been home for a while, but surely, this couldn't be his father? Where was the loud, robust, larger-than-life man he'd known and loved all his life? It couldn't be the frail and motionless person with his head covered in bandages lying in the bed in front of him.

Scrunching his eyes up tight, he took a moment before opening them, as if somehow he could change the appearance of the man before him. He pulled up the single chair that stood by his father's bed and accepted the realization that Duncan Munro was ill—gravely ill, from the look of the tubes and machines and other medical paraphernalia that crowded the small space around him.

He'd wanted to rant and rave about the injustice of his father's actions; he'd wanted to demand to know why; he'd wanted to bleat and bellow and shout out his anger, but he couldn't do any of those things to the feeble, old man in the bed. It looked like even a harsh whisper might do him in.

Feeling the need to reassure his father and perhaps even himself, he leaned over and took hold of his father's hand.

"Hi, Dad. It's Clayton. It's good to see you. It's been awhile. I've been flat out at work and all the other stuff we get caught up in. Ellie and the kids send their love."

He injected a lighter tone in his voice and continued. "The doctors and nurses say you're doing well, Dad. They're confident you're going to wake up." He paused and then spoke again with renewed determination. "Of *course* you're going to wake up. You're as tough as a piece of beef jerky. You've never let anything defeat you and this won't, either. I won't let it. You're going to pull through this, Dad. You wait and see."

His father remained quiet and unresponsive. Clayton's

shoulders slumped on a heavy sigh. He leaned forward with his head in his hands and recalled how angry he'd been since he heard about what happened. He was determined to believe the worst about the man he loved and respected beyond words.

How had he gotten to this point? When had he become so quick to judge? He prided himself on seeing things from all angles, on weighing up the evidence against the facts and then listening to his gut. It was the way he'd always worked and that had helped him become one of Australia's most respected criminal profilers.

Yet, here he was, with his father, no less, and he'd passed judgement against the man in a matter of moments. Clay might have had Declan on his side, but Tom and Brandon weren't. Even Riley had urged caution and his twin wasn't known to hold back.

Could it be the stress he was under at home? Could that be the reason he'd been so quick to lay blame? For the past six years, he'd walked a tightrope between Ellie, the wife he adored and loved with his heart and mind and body and soul, and his daughter, Olivia, the little girl he doted on. He'd taken pains not to take sides, not to lay blame when the two females in his life clashed. It happened with a depressing frequency.

All at once, he let his anger slide. "Oh, Dad," he confessed, "I don't know what the hell I'm going to do and I don't know how to fix it. I love Ellie to distraction. She's my life. But Olivia's my daughter, my little girl. I thought I was doing the right thing by marrying Ellie. I thought she might be the mother Olivia had never known. But I was wrong. I was absolutely wrong. Olivia thinks she's lost me, too. That I'm more into being Ellie's husband than being her father. Or at least, that's what she says."

He drew in a ragged breath. "I thought it would pass, that Olivia would get used to having Ellie around. I hoped they'd bond, but it's been six years and it still hasn't happened. Even when the boys came along, Olivia continued to keep her distance. I hate to admit it, but if anything, having

Mitchell and Damon has only made it worse. I thought we'd be one big, happy family, but the truth couldn't be any more different."

Clay lifted his head and stared at his father, but the man continued to lie unresponsive in the bed. With another sigh, he reached over and gave his father's hand a reassuring squeeze. Riley had urged him not to upset the man and here he was, dumping his problems at his father's feet. And not just little problems, either. At the moment, they seemed insurmountable.

Clay shook his head, despair weighing him down. Neither Ellie nor Olivia was going anywhere soon. He had to find a solution. He had to find a way for them to love each other, as dearly as he loved them both.

Duncan Munro struggled to hear his son's voice through the thick sludge that surrounded him. His head pounded and felt like it was stuffed full of wadding. He concentrated hard and was sure it was Clayton who spoke to him in a voice so full of desolation, it nearly broke his heart.

In the next moment, he thought it was Riley talking; the twins sounded so much alike. Without Caller ID, it was impossible to tell them apart when they called him on the phone. But then he caught mention of Ellie and Olivia and suddenly knew it was Clay.

Duncan listened to the pain in Clay's words and his chest went tight. He tried to turn his head, to open his mouth and offer comfort, but his brain refused to give the order. Nothing worked. He clenched his jaw in frustration. Or at least, he thought he did. His head was so foggy and dull, he couldn't be sure of anything anymore.

CHAPTER 15

Brandon
Grafton, New South Wales

Brandon strode out of the hospital and headed toward a garden on the edge of the entrance to the car park. Clayton's continued anger at their father upset him. The fact that Clay had fair reason to be angry made Brandon even sadder. He didn't want to believe his father was a cheat, but neither could he ignore what the evidence suggested.

What he wanted was to talk to his dad and have him allay his fears, like he always had in the past, but his dad was in a coma and no one knew when he'd wake; or even _if_ he'd wake...

Brandon missed Alex, too and the thought that she could go into labor any minute constantly played on his mind. He pulled out his phone and dialed his home number, needing to hear her voice.

In contrast to his heavy mood, the warm summer morning bathed him in its heat and the light breeze carried the heavy scent of jacarandas. The trees were famous for their thick clumps of purple bell-like flowers and there were several large specimens in the hospital grounds, their branches generously laden. He'd always loved the sight and the smell of them—an integral part of his childhood.

The huge trees lined many of the streets of Grafton and this time of year, the delicate, frondlike leaves were a bright, almost lime green, providing a stunning contrast to the spectacular purple display. The trees also clung to the banks of the wide Clarence River that ran along one side of the city and provided a haven for the millions of bats that called the jacarandas home.

Brandon remembered watching with awe as a kid while the evening sky filled with the black shadows of bats. By the thousands, they'd fly from somewhere upriver and settle among the dark branches. It was a nightly event he could almost set his watch by.

The phone was finally answered and Brandon swallowed a sigh of relief. If Alex was home, she wasn't in a labor ward and for that, he was inordinately grateful.

"Hi, sweetheart. It's me. I just thought I'd call you and see how you were doing."

"Brandon, how are you? How's your dad?"

"He-he's about the same, I think. I haven't been in to see him, yet. We got in too late last night and I just arrived at the hospital. Clayton's in with him now."

"I'm sure he'll be fine. You'll see. He's not going to give up easily. Where do you think you got your fighting spirit from?"

Brandon smiled at her compliment and hoped like hell she was right. "How are you doing? And the baby? No signs that it's on its way?"

"No, darling, I promise. My due date's still two days away and I'll probably go over, like the last time. If anything happens, I'll call you."

"Promise?"

Alex sighed. "I promise. Now, go and say hello to your father. You need to make sure he's all right."

"Thanks, babe. It's good to talk to you." He paused and then added in a voice thick with emotion, "I miss you."

"I miss you, too."

"Say hello to Sam and Bella and give them both a kiss."

"I will. I love you."

"I love you, too." Brandon ended the call and sighed.

Alex was right. It was time he went in and saw his father.

———————

Brandon glanced in the direction of the café that was situated on the ground floor of the hospital and spied Clayton and Riley in a queue of other customers who were waiting for their orders. Closing the distance between them, he touched Clay's arm to gain his attention.

"How're you doing?" he asked quietly.

Clay turned around and acknowledged him with a nod. "I'm okay. And Dad's no worse. I ran into Riley outside the ICU. We thought we'd grab a coffee. Do you want one?"

"Yeah, but I'll wait until after I've seen Dad." Brandon switched his attention to Riley and greeted him with a shake of the hand and a brotherly slap on the back. "It's good to see you, Riles."

"You, too, Bran. I take it you haven't been up there yet?"

"No, are they still letting visitors in?"

"Yeah, I think so. They didn't tell me anything different," Clay said.

"Good. I'll...I'll see you both in a little bit, then." He turned away.

"Brandon?"

He heard Clayton call out his name and slowly swung around to face him. "Yeah?"

"I'm sorry. For earlier. I shouldn't have spoken to you like that."

Brandon shrugged. "Don't sweat it, bro. We're all doing it tough at the moment. None of us saw this coming. We're all trying to deal with it the best way we can."

Relief softened the hard lines of Clayton's face. "Yeah, well, thanks for understanding. I was an asshole and I should have known better."

Brandon patted his brother on the back. "He's on the third floor, right?"

Clayton nodded. "Right down the end of the corridor."

"I'll see you shortly then," Brandon said and then added, "I'll have a cappuccino in a mug, no sugar."

Clayton smiled softly and Brandon headed toward the elevators.

A young nurse with a bouncy, blond ponytail buzzed him through the doors of the ICU and met him on the other side.

"Your father's right this way," she said and he followed her into the ward. Her rubber-soled shoes made no noise on the shiny, cream-colored linoleum. Mindful of the other patients, he did his best to keep the sound of his boots on the floor to a minimum.

"He's a popular man this morning," the nurse mused. "You're the third visitor he's had today."

"I guess you saw a couple of my brothers," Brandon replied. "There are seven of us all together."

Her eyebrows rose in surprise. "Seven sons? Wow!"

"No, not seven sons," he corrected. "Five sons and two daughters."

The nurse grinned. "That's still wow!"

He smiled back at her. She was slim and pretty and a long time ago, he probably would have been interested. But that was before Alex.

"Here he is. I've just given him a wash. He still hasn't regained consciousness, but it's early days yet. Besides, that's not a bad thing. It gives his body a chance to heal."

Brandon edged closer to the bed and stared down at his father and tried to contain his surprise. The nurse's voice faded away. He'd expected him to look ill—and he did. What he hadn't expected was to see him look so helpless.

Taking a seat in the hard plastic chair by the bed, he leaned over and gave his father a kiss. His cheek was rough beneath Brandon's lips. His dad was badly in need of a shave. Even a day's worth of stubble was noticeable and left a dark shadow along his father's jawline. His skin, usually burnished dark gold from his aboriginal heritage, was now almost as white as the sheets. Brandon stifled a surge of panic and took hold of his father's hand.

"Hello Dad, it's me. Brandon. It's good to see you.

You're... You're looking good. Don't worry, you're going to be fine. This isn't the end, not by a long shot. You're bigger and stronger than that and you never run away from a fight." He paused and dragged in a breath. "We all love you, Dad, but we need some answers. No one wants to believe you'd cheat on Mom. We just want you to tell us what happened."

The respirator continued to do its monotonous job, filling his father's lungs with air and then deflating them. Watching the rhythmic rise and fall of his chest, Brandon prayed that the words he spoke were true. He wasn't ready to lose his father. He didn't know if he'd ever be ready, but he couldn't let him go like this. With so much hurt and confusion and pain and so many unanswered questions.

He squeezed his father's hand again and continued to fill the silence. "The baby's due in two days, Dad. Alex is counting down. She's had about enough of this pregnancy. It took a bit more out of her this time. I guess she's that much older, too. I'm worried about the labor. She had such a hard time of it when Bella was born. I can't stand to think of it happening again."

He sighed. "I want Alex to have a C-section, but she won't hear of it. She says it's better for her and the baby this way, but hell, I'm not so sure. She wasn't the one having panic attacks the last time whenever Bella's heart rate fell below eighty. I thought I was going to lose them both. I've never been so scared in my life, even when I was working undercover in Jakarta, infiltrating terrorist cells."

He dragged in another breath. "I-I can't lose them, Dad. I just can't. Alex is my life. And the baby..." He shook his head. "I used to think my career was all that mattered. I used to think I didn't have the time or the inclination to be responsible for a child. Then, I found out about Sam and how much Alex still loved me and everything changed. Now we have Bella and another one on the way and I couldn't be happier. It's just the birth that terrifies me."

He released his father's hand and leaned back in the chair. "I guess you understand. You went through it seven times. At least, I think you did. Things were a bit different in your day; they didn't always let dads into the birthing suite. Maybe that was a good thing? But I guess the stress and anxiety and the *waiting* would have been just the same."

Brandon ran a hand through his hair and thought of all the times his father had been there for him. During his teenage years, his struggles with puberty were made even more complicated by issues pertaining to his mixed heritage. There was a brief time when he was nearly eighteen that he didn't feel like he fit into either world: not the black world of his father or white world of his mother. It had taken the wisdom and love of his parents and many countless discussions with his father deep into the night to make him see and believe he fit into *both* worlds and it would always be that way, for as long as he wanted it to be.

He didn't want to believe his dad had been unfaithful, despite the evidence that had been found. His father had been his role model, his inspiration, his yardstick for the way he lived his life. He refused to accept that the man he believed in and loved beyond measure could ever do something so hurtful, so dishonest. He sent a desperate, silent prayer heavenwards that his father would wake and explain it all away. The time couldn't come soon enough.

Duncan felt the whisper softness of Brandon's lips against his cheek and sighed. He hadn't seen his third oldest boy for way too long. The lives of his children were so busy these days and most of them lived too far away.

If it had been up to him, he'd have had them all living in Grafton, close enough so that he could see them and spend time with them whenever he chose. The years sped by far too quickly; they were going by in a blur. He couldn't keep up with everyone and everything. Life was too damned short.

He knew Brandon was worried about the impending birth

of his child. He'd spoken to him about it before. He and Marguerite had been sick with worry the last time, when Brandon had called to tell them Alex's labor hadn't been going well. She'd been in labor for ten hours by then and the doctors were concerned. The baby was too big for her pelvis. Brandon hadn't been able to keep the panic out of his voice.

Duncan understood exactly how his son was feeling. He'd spent many a tense hour outside a delivery suite. He'd been lucky that most of Marguerite's labors had been short and uneventful, but he could still remember his fear when he was told the twins were in trouble.

It had been more than thirty-three years ago, but he could remember it like it was yesterday. Riley was in the lead and had gotten stuck in the birth canal. Both babies were at risk. It had been too late for a C-section. The door to the delivery room had swung open and closed more times than he could count. More and more medical staff filled the room, their faces more and more concerned. All Duncan could do was pray.

In the end, it had turned our all right. When Riley and Clayton had been born fit and healthy, Duncan had been weak with relief and oh, so very grateful. It had been fortunate the rest of Marguerite's births had given no one cause to panic. He didn't know how he would have coped with another medical emergency where the lives of his family were at risk.

He had a bucketload of sympathy for Brandon's predicament and more than a little understanding. All he could do was hope for the best and pray that both Alex and the unborn child would come out of it okay.

He sighed and thought of his wife and wondered if she'd stopped by. He didn't know how long he'd been there, but if his sons were near, it must have been more than a few hours. He hoped she'd visit him soon. He was tired and wanted to sleep. But he missed her with a vengeance and wanted to see her even more.

CHAPTER 16

Josie
Grafton Base Hospital

Josie stepped through the double sliding doors and inside the foyer of the Grafton Base Hospital. A beautifully decorated Christmas tree, complete with brightly wrapped presents piled high beneath it, almost filled an entire corner. Not far away, a group of people dressed in choir robes sang joyful Christmas carols, reminding her that it was only a matter of days away. Glancing sideways, she smiled in pleasure when she spied three of her older brothers at the nearby café.

"Clayton! Riley! Brandon!" She walked over to where they sat at a table and greeted them. The men pushed away from their table, stood and returned her embrace. Josie turned to Riley.

"It's good to see you, Riles. You're looking fit and healthy. It feels like forever since I've been home. How are Kate and the twins?"

"You're looking good, too, little sister. The Big Smoke of Brisbane agrees with you. Kate is as happy and serene as ever, the girls are little terrors." He shrugged and added a smile. "Nothing's new."

"You love them and you know it," she replied, not believing his gripe about the twins for an instant.

"Of course I do," he replied. "But that doesn't mean I wouldn't like to strangle them every now and again." Riley softened his words with another smile and Josie addressed Clayton and Brandon.

"You left early this morning."

"Not really. Who'd have thought you could sleep so long? It's good to see you up at last, little sis," Brandon teased and ruffled her long blond hair.

Josie poked out her tongue and then grinned. After getting in late the night before and then spending time catching up with everyone, she'd overslept. By the time she made it to the kitchen, Tom and Declan were on their way out and Clayton and Brandon had already left. Her mother was also keen to return to her husband's side, but knowing that his visitors would probably still be restricted, she'd graciously agreed to wait until her children had seen him. Chanel opted to wait with her. Josie felt no such patience.

Instead, she'd rushed to catch a ride with her brothers. There hadn't been time to deal with her hair and pull the thick mane back into the sensible bun she normally favored. She barely had enough time to grab a coffee from the pot her mother had made earlier.

The boys returned to their seats. Josie snagged a chair from the next table and squeezed in between Riley and Brandon.

"How did you get here?" Clayton asked.

Josie grimaced. "I caught a lift with Tom and Declan. I should have taken my own car or waited to ride with Chanel and Mom. Those boys did nothing but argue the whole way. Declan's convinced of Dad's guilt and Tom feels equally sure about his innocence. Anyone would think they were lawyers, the way they've been at each other's throats, standing guard at opposite ends of the bar table and refusing to concede the other might have a point."

Clayton and Brandon shared a guilty look. Josie frowned. "What? Not you, too? How *could* you? How could you think Dad's guilty of cheating? You two know him even better than I do!"

"Hey, don't blame me," Brandon protested. "I'm not the one who had him tarred and feathered."

She turned a disappointed gaze on Clayton. "Not *you*, Clay? You climb into people's minds for a living! How could you jump to such a conclusion about your own father without any proof?"

Her brothers exchanged a look. Josie was immediately suspicious. Sudden fear that she might not like what she was about to hear held her immobile. Her gaze shifted from one man to the other. "What is it, boys? What haven't I been told?"

"It depends," Clayton muttered.

Josie blew out a breath of exasperation. "On what?"

"On what Mom told you," Brandon added.

Josie sucked in a deep breath and released it slowly. "Mom told me Dad had been found unconscious in a hotel room and the police thought he might have been meeting a woman there. I assumed it wasn't his wife," she finished, her voice dry. "Of course, I barely paid it any mind. As if Dad would be cheating on Mom, huh? The very idea's ridiculous."

Her brothers shared another look and Josie's dread increased. Now she *really* didn't know if she wanted to hear what they had to say. "What? What is it? Why are you all looking at me like that?"

"Josie," Clayton said, "the police found some...things."

She frowned. "What kind of things?"

Riley blew out his breath on a heavy sigh. Color tinged his cheeks. "Candles, massage oils, champagne glasses...lingerie."

Josie gasped, her own cheeks burning, in both embarrassment and disbelief. "L-lingerie? You're kidding me, right?"

Brandon shook his head and avoided her gaze. "I'm afraid not, sis."

Josie pushed away from the table, her mind full of confusion. Her mother had glossed over the conclusions the police had drawn and Josie had done much the same.

She'd been more focused on the frightening news that her father was now in a coma.

He'd been the stalwart being of her childhood: tall, strong and dependable. There was nothing he couldn't do and there was nothing he couldn't fix. As she grew older, knowing he was the first aboriginal District Court Judge in New South Wales had been an immense source of pride and inspiration. She'd grown into adulthood knowing she had his support in whatever career path she chose and she also knew she had his unconditional love.

And there it was: The overriding feeling that permeated every memory from her childhood and even later, was love. The love between her father and mother was almost palpable; everyone knew about it; no one questioned it. It just *was*.

Now she had to face the possibility that it had all been a façade. Her father had been found in a hotel room with sex paraphernalia. Candles, oils, champagne, lingerie...

Josie's heart rebelled at the thought of her father being unfaithful, but her head forced her to give it some consideration. The police who had attended the scene had drawn that conclusion. They'd been trained to observe and make calculated, logical assumptions on the evidence presented to them. *Could it be true?* Could her father have been leading some kind of double life?

She shuddered at the thought and tried not to think about the numerous stories she'd read and heard about in trashy magazines and even trashier TV programs. Okay, it had happened before. Some people deceived their family like that, but not her father. *Surely, not her father?*

Josie's shoulders slumped under the weight of her thoughts. She glanced over at her brothers and her heart tugged at the almost identical expressions of fear and concern on their faces. Clayton had always been the more pragmatic of them: weighing up the facts and then arriving at a decision. Brandon tended to react more from the heart. He was much more like Riley that way.

She compressed her lips and blew out her breath, wishing

the issue would simply go away. *How could you, Dad?* The thought was almost immediately followed with a denial. *He couldn't have.*

"I'm going up to visit Dad," she said, suddenly needing to see him. "I-I'll catch up with you a little later." She pushed away from the table and collected her handbag. Brandon stood with her and gave her a quick, hard hug.

"Are you okay?" he murmured.

Emotion burned behind her eyes and she blinked hard to keep the tears at bay. "Yes. I-I'm fine."

"I'm sorry you had to find out like that. We probably shouldn't have told you."

"No, I'm glad you did. I assume everyone else knows?"

"I'm not sure about Chanel, but yes, the rest of us do."

Josie bit her lip and averted her gaze. She knew without being told how agonizing the news was to all of her siblings, including the brothers that watched her now with concern and kindness in their eyes.

"Have you seen him today?" she asked.

"Yes," Brandon responded. "We all have."

"How is he?"

Brandon's lips tightened. "He's okay. No change, but that's a good thing, according to the nurses." He paused and then asked, "How are you getting home?"

She grimaced. "The same way I came in, I guess, with Tom and Declan."

"You can always get a ride with us. We're happy to wait for you, aren't we Clay?"

Clayton nodded. "Of course. They won't let you stay too long with Dad, anyway. They're still restricting visits to less than ten minutes."

"I'd better get moving, then. Thanks for the offer. Who knows whether Tom and Declan have calmed down enough yet to be civil toward one another? If you don't mind waiting, I think I'd prefer to ride home with you."

Brandon smiled. "No trouble at all, little sis. We're happy to be of service."

———————

The quiet *swoosh* of the respirators and the beeps and hums of the other equipment surrounding the patients in the ICU was a little unnerving and Josie forced herself forward with more than a little trepidation. Despite her career as a child psychologist, she'd always had a fear of hospitals. Knowing her father was lying gravely ill in a bed in the ICU was almost enough to bring on a panic attack.

A moment later, the nurse nodded toward the patient in the next bed and Josie's thoughts scattered like dandelions on the breeze. She bit back a sob.

He was so pale, she wondered for a second whether he'd died. Then, his chest rose imperceptibly and lowered just as much and the breath she'd been holding came out in a rush. With dread weighing down her feet, she closed the distance between them and immediately reached for his hand.

"Oh, Dad! You poor, poor thing! It's Josie. I've come to say hello. What in heaven's name have you been doing to yourself?" Her gaze skittered away from the bandages that were wrapped around his head. Lifting his gnarled, old hand, she pressed it against her cheek. The warmth of his skin reassured her, but his lack of response both alarmed and saddened her. She couldn't bear to think about the possibility that he might never wake up; that he could remain in this state of…nothingness for the rest of his life. Or worse, that he could die.

Refusing to contemplate either possibility, she tugged the nearby chair close to the bed. Taking a seat, she tightened her fingers around her father's hand and tried to think of something else to say. She'd read in a medical journal that it was possible for people in a coma to still be cognizant of their surroundings. It was important she think of something positive to tell him; something for him to focus on; something to lift his spirits.

"I hate my job, Dad. I want to quit." The words fell out of

her mouth. *So much for trying to cheer him up; so much for something positive. What the hell am I thinking?*

Now that she'd blurted her thoughts aloud, she realized how true they were and how long they'd been pushing to be heard. She did hate her job. It was nothing like she'd thought it would be. After all the years of study, she couldn't believe how disappointed and uninspired she was with the reality of working as a child psychologist.

"It's not the work itself," she added, turning to her father. "It's the patients, or more specifically, their parents. "I'm working in a private practice in an incredibly nice part of town. My office is spacious and has a view of the river. I'm earning a decent income and my work colleagues are pleasant and friendly, but the parents are driving me *nuts!* They're all the same; too much money and not enough common sense."

She dragged in a breath and took heart from the silent encouragement offered by the man in the bed. As if a dam wall had been breached, she continued. "They think if they pay a fortune in therapy, it's going to make up for the years of parental neglect, the years when they were too busy earning another million or three to even take notice of their kids. The kids have every material possession most kids want and need. What they *really* want, what they really *need* is for their parents to acknowledge they exist. They want parents who are there for them after school or when they're going to bed. They want parents who remember it's their dance recital and who care enough to attend; they want parents who won't just give them money, but who will give them a slice of their time."

She shook her head. "These people don't seem to get it. They ask me in confused desperation what could possibly be wrong with their little girl and why their child is behaving like this or like that, when the answer's staring them in the face. When I try to explain the problem and—heaven forbid— offer the simple solution, they don't want to know. They don't want to have to confront the possibility that their lifestyle has to change, that their priorities need to be reassessed, that they have to find time for their offspring."

Her breath came faster. The more her anger rose, the tighter she squeezed her father's fingers. With a startled gasp, she realized what she was doing and immediately loosened her hold. Gently now, she let his hand fall back to the sheet and was horrified to notice his fingers were white from the pressure.

"I'm sorry, Dad," she murmured, her voice more on an even keel. "I shouldn't have dumped all of that on you. I guess I had some vision in my head of how wonderful it would be when I graduated and was able to have contact with real live patients and help them overcome the obstacles in their lives. All I've managed is to upset most of them and I've completely alienated their parents. My boss isn't happy and I don't know what to do. It's not what I signed up for, Dad."

She looked across at his silent form and tears suddenly crowded her eyes. All her life, he'd been there for her, offering her a shoulder to cry on, listening to her tale of woes, offering heartfelt, sensible advice. She wasn't ready to let that go; she wasn't ready to let *him* go.

And she'd only known him for twenty-eight years. She couldn't even begin to imagine how it felt for her mother.

Duncan grimaced at the tourniquet that threatened to cut off the blood flow to his hand and tried to focus on the words that fell from his oldest daughter's lips. The anger, the pain, the disillusionment that weighed down her conversation pulled at his heart. He wanted to be able to tell her everything was all right, that nothing was ever so bad it couldn't be fixed, but once again, his brain refused to cooperate.

Frustration surged through him and he groaned beneath his breath. He was through with this inability to communicate, with the struggle of being heard. He wanted to shout and scream and yell. He wanted people to take notice.

Josie was speaking again and her voice was clouded with tears. He hated that she was hurting; he hated even more that he couldn't offer her comfort. There was nothing he could do.

CHAPTER 17

Tom
Grafton Base Hospital

Tom watched Declan storm off through the hospital car park, the same way Josie had done earlier, but instead of heading toward the hospital entrance, he strode off in the opposite direction. Tom bit down on a sigh. They'd been arguing since they left home about whether or not their father was an adulterer. Only now, with his brother's abrupt departure, the argument had come to a halt.

Tom refused to believe his father had been unfaithful, no matter what Riley's detective mates said. *They had it wrong.* His father might have been found in what could be construed as a compromising situation, but Tom simply refused to believe it was true.

At thirty-eight years old and the eldest Munro sibling, he'd known his father for longer than any of the others. Okay, so Declan was only two years younger, but those two years counted for a lot. Anyone could tell you that. Besides, his mother didn't believe it, either. She'd said as much to them the night before.

Declan had argued in the car that of course she was standing by him, he wouldn't expect anything else, but Tom was having none of it. His mother was fiercely loyal to her husband, but not to the point of stupidity. If she truly believed he was guilty, she wouldn't have been so determined to convince them of his innocence. Besides, she'd been married to the man for forty years. No one knew him better than she did.

With a sigh and a shake of his head, Tom headed toward the hospital entrance and stepped inside the foyer. He was met with a rush of cool air and welcomed the feel of it after the stifling heat from outside. It was nearing midday and the summer sun had made its presence felt.

An enormous Christmas tree decorated with golden fairy lights and blue and silver themed baubles filled one corner of the entryway and reminded him that Christmas was getting closer. His thoughts went to Lily and the kids and then circled back to his father. He could only hope he would recover and be home with them by then. No one loved Christmas more than his dad. Who knew? He might even be waking up now?

Keeping the positive thought at the forefront of his mind, he strode past the café on his way toward the elevators.

"Tom!"

Swinging around, he spied three of his brothers and Josie seated at a table, mugs of coffee and plates of sandwiches laid out in front of them.

"Hey, guys. How are you all? I was just on my way to see Dad."

"You're nearly too late," Clayton said. "Visiting hours finish at twelve."

Tom glanced at his watch, but knew it was almost midday. He'd been too wrapped up in his argument with Declan to give the visiting hours a moment's thought. He cursed under his breath.

Josie threw him a pointed look. "Where's Declan?" she asked, as if she could read his mind.

Tom shrugged and looked away. "Who knows?"

"You two aren't *still* fighting, are you?" Brandon asked, shaking his head.

"Well, wouldn't you?" Tom retorted, feeling his face grow hot. "Declan's convinced Dad was doing the dirty on Mom.

He refuses to consider the evidence might be wrong or, at the very least, misconstrued. He's a cop. He's been trained to look past the obvious. It's annoying the hell out of me that he won't."

Clayton's bark of laughter was loud enough to turn the heads of a few of the other diners. Josie shot him a look of embarrassment.

"Will you keep it down?" she hissed, her gaze moving from Clayton and Tom and encompassed Brandon and Riley. "People are looking at us."

Brandon lifted his hands in surrender. "Hey, it wasn't me! Save your chastisement for them!" He indicated Tom and Clayton with his head. "They're the ones drawing all the attention."

Josie turned her glare on the brothers in question. "He's right. Now, Tom, if you want to visit Dad, you'd better hurry. I just came from there. He's doing okay, no change, apparently. Just be prepared for..." Her words faded off.

Tom frowned. "For what? What are you talking about?"

Josie looked around at her other brothers. None of them met her gaze. Tom did his best to ignore the fear that coiled deep in his gut. "What aren't you telling me, people? What's the matter with Dad?"

"Nothing's the matter with him," Josie answered a little impatiently. "Well, apart from the fact he had an aneurysm rupture in his brain, emergency surgery and is now in a coma. It's just that..." She hesitated once again.

"Spit it out, Josie!" Tom growled. She sighed and looked to Brandon for help.

"It's just that he looks so old and helpless," Brandon said. "And his head is covered in bandages. There are tubes coming out every which way and...I-I think that was a shock to all of us." He gazed around the group at the table. "I wasn't expecting to see him like that. He's always been so...so *alive*, so *present* and now...now he's lost something."

Tom stared at his siblings and tried to process Brandon's words, but right at that moment, they were beyond him. His father had always been larger than life. It was impossible to imagine him any different. With a heavy sigh, he murmured farewells to his siblings and continued to the elevators.

His mother had told him the ICU was on level three. He drew in a deep breath and squared his shoulders, readying himself for what was to come.

———————

It was the smell of antiseptic that Tom noticed first—that and the almost eerie stillness of the patients that filled all of the beds. He followed the nurse in silence, looking neither left nor right. She'd warned him that visiting hours were over and that he'd have to make it quick. He'd explained he'd flown from Sydney and expressed his gratitude that she allowed him in.

A moment later, he spied the large form of his father. The sight might have shocked him if Josie and Brandon hadn't warned him. He'd never seen his father look so lifeless. His skin blended into the sheets, almost as white as the bandages around his head. The slackness of his jaw was also alarming. The fact that there was no hint of a response when Tom greeted him was even more so. The only sign of life Tom could discern was the slight rise and fall of his father's chest.

Setting his jaw against his panic, Tom leaned over and clasped his father's hand. His fingers lay puffy and limp and unresponsive and Tom's heart clenched with pain and fear. According to Declan, his father's brain was still responding, but Tom couldn't help but wonder how accurate the reports were.

Surely, if his father's brain still worked, he'd feel Tom's touch, hear his greeting, even if he couldn't offer a response? And yet, there was nothing: Not the slightest flicker of an eyelid, or the movement of his hand, to indicate he had any clue his oldest child was there.

Despair crept through Tom's veins and he did his best to hold it in. *He was being stupid.* His father wasn't dead. Far from it.

He quickly averted his gaze and stared steadfastly at a spot across the room and tried desperately to convince himself it was true. A different nurse from the one who had let him in, materialized in his peripheral vision carrying a clipboard under her arm. He turned to look at her, grateful for the distraction. She was young and attractive and offered him an apologetic smile.

"Hi, I'm Bridie. I'm looking after your father today. I'm sorry to interrupt your visit, but I need to check his vitals. I won't be a minute."

Tom made to leave, but she hastened to reassure him it wasn't necessary. He pulled the solitary chair well away from the bed and sat and watched while she took his father's temperature. She checked each one of the machines that were keeping his father alive and then recorded various entries on her paper. A few moments later, she looked across at him and smiled once again.

"Okay, we're all done."

"How is he?"

"He's stable, so that's a good sign. He still has a little swelling on the brain from the aneurysm bleed, so it's not unusual for him to remain unconscious. I'm sure once the swelling goes down, we'll see a marked improvement."

Hope surged through him. "How long will it take?"

The nurse lifted a slender shoulder in a half shrug. Her ponytail swayed with the movement. "It depends. A lot of patients will regain consciousness within a day or so. Sometimes, it takes a little longer. We'll just have to wait and see."

Tom swallowed a sigh and tried not to look disheartened. He could tell the nurse was doing all she could to cheer him up. A moment later, she collected her notes and moved away. He murmured his thanks and she shot him a look filled with understanding.

"He's going to be okay," she said. "It's nearly Christmas. There's no way he's not going to wake up in time for that. I won't have it any other way and neither will Santa." She winked at him.

A reluctant grin tugged at Tom's lips. She smiled back and he was reminded of Lily and the way she looked when she was trying to rouse him from his doldrums. At the thought of his wife, his smile slowly faded. He hadn't been gone twenty-four hours and already he missed her. It was ridiculous. They'd been married for fifteen years. He should be able to spend a night away from her without pining like an idiot.

The nurse had slipped away, unnoticed. He dragged the chair closer to the bed until he was within reach of the man he'd been proud and honored to call Dad for the whole of his life.

"Hey, Dad. It's Tom. How are you doing?"

Tom grimaced as soon as the words left his mouth. *What a stupid question.* His father had suffered a bleed on the brain and was still in a coma. How the hell did he think he was doing?

He cleared his throat and tried again. "They told us where they found you, Dad. I want you to know, I don't believe what they're saying. I don't believe it for an instant. You can't be having an affair. It isn't possible. You love Mom too much. You love all of us too much to betray us like that. I refuse to believe it. There has to be another explanation."

Tom's breath came fast and he purposefully worked to slow it down. He thought of his children—Cassie and Joe—and prayed that his faith in his father wasn't misplaced. Even though they were now both teenagers, they still idolized their grandfather. They'd be just as devastated as the rest of the family if Tom's instincts were off the mark.

He hadn't breathed a word of the police findings to anyone back home, not even to Lily, when he phoned her last night. He'd devoted his entire adult life to law enforcement and believed with every fiber of his being that a man was entitled to the presumption of innocence. Extending that belief to his father was the very least he could do.

His thoughts returned to his children and he frowned, wanting so much to tell his father about Cassie and to seek his advice.

"Cassie's going through a difficult phase, Dad. She turned sixteen a few months ago and I don't know if it's an age thing or if there is something more to it. She's always been an A-grade student, but for the last six months, her marks have been slipping. She's become more and more withdrawn. It's so unlike my sunny, little girl, Dad. I don't know what's wrong with her."

His father didn't respond, but Tom continued, anyway. It felt better to tell his father about it, even if his dad appeared not to hear.

"Lily keeps telling me to ignore it; that she'll outgrow it, but her bad behaviour is escalating and I'm getting really worried. It's gone well beyond a "phase," as far as I'm concerned. The problem is, I don't have a clue what to do about it. The very thought of disciplining her floods me with guilt. It's only been a little over three years since…since she was abducted by that pedophile."

He shuddered at the memory. "Thank Christ she was spared the horror of a rape, but still, I can't begin to imagine the unspeakable terror she must have gone through. It's no wonder the trauma of it stayed with her for such a long time, despite the hundreds of hours of therapy.

"A year or so ago, I thought she'd turned the corner and I breathed a grateful sigh of relief. We all did. Cassie was more and more like my beautiful, carefree daughter of the past. She seemed to have conquered her nightmares. But lately, it's like she's regressed. I don't know if it has anything to do with what she experienced when she was younger, or if it's merely a normal teenage rebellious phase, like Lily seems to think. That's the problem, Dad. I just don't know. I want to help her. I want to help my baby smile again, but I don't know how to do it."

His voice hitched and tears welled up in his eyes. He was a veteran police negotiator who'd faced down countless scenes that would strike terror in the hearts of lesser men, but the thought of his beautiful daughter, sad and withdrawn and becoming more so by the day brought him to his knees.

"I guess I have to trust Lily's judgement, Dad. As a school

teacher, she deals with kids and their problems all the time. She knows how they react and interact. I just hope she's right about Cassie. I miss my little girl. I want her back."

A sob caught in the back of his throat and he swallowed hard and focused on something happier. *Joe.* Three years younger than Cassie, he was the best kid a father could want. Always joking, always laughing, he'd never given them a moment's trouble. He'd only just hit puberty with all its problems and pitfalls, but Tom was confident his son would come through it without a hitch. The kid faced any challenge with confidence and determination. Tom wished he could say the same about himself.

He grimaced and rubbed at the familiar, small lump through his T-shirt. It was right below his nipple and had been there for months. After having seen his mother fight breast cancer, he ought to have known better than to ignore it, but the truth was, it frightened the hell out of him.

Besides, he'd been busy at work and then at home. With Lily returning to part-time study and taking her courses at night, he just hadn't found the time to go and see someone about it. Twice now, he'd made and cancelled doctors' appointments, including the one he'd cancelled to fly up to Grafton.

A part of him was sure he was better off not knowing. *What if it is cancer?* What if it were terminal? Breast cancer in men was rare, but every now and then it happened. What if he died? How would Lily survive on one income? There was his life insurance, of course, but would it be enough? And then there were his kids. How would they cope without a father?

Tom's chest tightened with emotion. His jaw clenched with the effort of holding it all in. Then, he swore quietly under his breath.

He was being ridiculous. It was probably nothing—a cyst, or perhaps, a tumor that was benign. He ought to do himself and his family a favor and get the damned thing checked out. It was the sensible thing to do. Then he would know for sure and he could stop thinking such stupid thoughts and conjuring up wild scenarios of death and devastation.

He glanced back at his father and shook his head. "Christ, Dad, I'm sorry. What sort of comfort am I? You're the one lying unconscious and I'm here worrying about myself. I should be telling you funny jokes and making sure you're fighting to pull through instead of making it all about me. Talk about selfish! You should be chewing my ear out, like you would be if you were awake."

His voice hitched again and a wave of longing washed over him. *What he wouldn't give to have his father open up his eyes and say hello.* He tightened his fingers around the gnarled, old hand and then bent and pressed a kiss against his knuckles. He didn't know what his father had done or not done, but whatever it was, they'd work through it. Nothing would change the love he felt for the man who'd loved his children unconditionally and been such an integral and inspirational part of his life.

He drew in a deep breath and eased it out. With his lips moving silently, he sent up a prayer that all of them would be all right.

———————

Duncan listened to Tom's heartfelt words and struggled to break free of the weight that held him down. The pain in his firstborn's voice was almost more than he could bear. He wanted to draw him into his arms and comfort him like he used to when Tom was young, but the ache in his chest and the fog in his head refused to release him. The frustration nearly made him cry out and he would have, if he could.

The knowledge that some people had drawn the logical conclusion he was having an affair didn't come as any real surprise. He thought back to his preparations and couldn't blame them for arriving at that point. It pained him to think some of his family might also think that and he could only pray that, like Tom, his wife wasn't among them.

The thought of Marguerite sent another pang racing through him. He needed her by his side. He needed her gentle touch. He needed her to soothe away the pain and to reassure him everything was going to be all right. The pounding in his head hadn't lessened and he was terrified it never would.

Where was she?

CHAPTER 18

Declan
Grafton, New South Wales

Declan jammed his hands in his pockets and kicked at the loose stones on the well-marked gravel path that skirted the bank of the Clarence River. The wide expanse of water sparkled in the afternoon sun, sending shards of light dancing across the surface, but he was mostly oblivious to its beauty.

He'd stormed away from Tom after failing to convince his oldest brother yet again that the facts didn't lie. *Tom should know better.* He'd been a cop longer than any of them. None of them wanted to believe their father had been cheating, but the evidence plainly indicated it was true.

It was just like he'd yelled at Tom: The facts didn't lie. There was no other possible reason for his father to be in a hotel room with champagne, roses, massage oils and lingerie and not be expecting a woman. It was ridiculous to think otherwise and Tom darn well knew it. So what if the woman hadn't surfaced? If it had been any other man but their father, no one would have questioned the evidence. It was just that the man involved was their much loved and admired father. It was only for that reason they'd forced themselves to voice their sometimes heated denials.

Declan had wanted to voice his, too. It had been his first instinct when Clayton had told him, but no matter which way he looked at it, the facts remained the same. It infuriated him that Tom stubbornly refused to see.

His phone vibrated against his chest and he tugged it out. He'd turned it on silent in anticipation of entering the hospital, but so far, he hadn't been able to calm down enough to go in. Glancing at the screen, he couldn't help but smile. *It was Chloe.*

He'd spoken to her the night before, but the phone call had been brief. She'd been tired and distracted and he'd heard Jessie crying in the background. It hadn't been the time to tell her the truth about his father, no matter how much he wanted to. But now, it was all he could do not to blurt it out the moment he answered her call.

Instead, he drew in a deep breath and greeted her with a smile. "Hello, gorgeous wife. What are you up to?"

Chloe giggled. "Hello, yourself. You're sounding a little more chipper this morning. I take it your father's awake?"

Declan immediately sobered, his belly once again churning with dread. "No, at least, not that I know of. I haven't seen him, yet."

The laughter in Chloe's voice faded. "Declan, what do you mean, you haven't seen him yet? The day's half over."

He squeezed his eyes shut and pinched the bridge of his nose. "Yeah, it is and I think the morning visiting hours are, too. I'll have to wait until this afternoon to see him."

"What's the matter, Declan? What's happened?"

He heard the fear and confusion in her voice and hastened to reassure her. "It's nothing. I'm fine. Well, it's not nothing, but it has nothing to do with *me*."

"Talk to me, darling. Please. Something's not right."

Declan's shoulders slumped on a heavy sigh. Up ahead of him, he spied an empty park bench and made his way over to it. He threw himself down and sighed again. "You're right. There's no other way to tell you this, so I'm going to say it straight out: Dad's been having an affair."

"What?" Chloe's shocked response reverberated deep inside him.

"I didn't want to believe it, either, but the evidence was there in plain view. Dad was found in a hotel room. The police who attended the scene told Riley what they found. While there was no woman there, apparently it was more than obvious he'd been expecting one and it sure as hell wasn't my mother."

"I don't believe it," Chloe murmured, her voice still laced with shock. "What kind of things did they find?"

Declan rattled off the items as quickly as he could. Every time he thought about them, his anger and embarrassment bubbled higher.

Chloe remained silent. A moment later, she spoke slowly, as if choosing her words with care. "Things aren't always as they appear, Declan."

His temper leaped into life. "Oh, come on! Not you, too! It is what it is! The facts don't lie. Why am I the only one who has the guts to acknowledge it?"

"All I'm saying is that I don't think you should be so quick to jump to conclusions. Okay, I hear what you're saying and it certainly doesn't look good, but I remember a time only a couple of years ago when I was also convinced the facts didn't lie."

Declan's jaw clenched and he breathed in deeply, forcing the air out of his nose. She was referring to the time he'd been wrongly accused of illegally accessing child pornography. She'd been the senior Internal Affairs Investigator on his case and all of the facts had pointed to his guilt. If it hadn't been for his own belief in his innocence and Chloe's dogged determination to look behind the obvious, he'd have been convicted of a heinous crime—a crime he hadn't committed.

He bit his lip and conceded her point. His father hadn't done anything illegal, but the principle was just the same. When Declan had been under the spotlight, his father had been nothing but supportive. In fact, Declan wouldn't have withstood the turmoil and devastation the whole situation wrought, without his father's unwavering belief in his innocence, despite the overwhelming evidence to the contrary.

Declan bent over at the waist, suddenly flooded with guilt. He, of all people, should have known better. He knew firsthand what it felt like to be presumed guilty without ever having been given the chance to set the record straight. If it hadn't been for Chloe's persistence, the truth might never have come out.

His father was in a coma and was in no shape or form to defend himself. He was relying on his wife and family to come to his defense in his hour of need, to believe in his innocence no matter what the evidence dictated. And Declan had let him down. A sob caught in Declan's throat and his chest heaved.

"Oh, Christ, Chloe. You're right. How could I have been so stupid? How could I have been so blind? My cop instincts kicked in and I refused to consider any other possibility. He's my *father!* How could I forget his loyalty? How could I forget his love? I'm a complete and utter jerk. And Tom. Shit, the things I said to Tom." He shook his head, burning with shame.

"It's okay, Declan. It's okay. I'm sure Tom understands. You've all had a tremendous shock. Apart from discovering your father might or might not have been unfaithful, he's lying in a coma and no one knows whether he'll come out of it. I think everyone will forgive you for being a little...irrational. They love you, after all. Almost as much as I do."

His heart filled with tenderness and he swallowed the lump in his throat. "Thank you, sweetheart. I really needed to hear that. I love you so much it hurts."

"I know what you mean," Chloe whispered.

Declan sat up and drew in a deep breath and then blew the air out on a sigh. "I owe Tom an apology."

"Yes, darling, you do."

"I need to see Dad. I owe him an apology, too."

"I'm sure he'll understand."

"Christ, Chloe, what would I do without you?"

"I'm not going anywhere and neither are the kids."

Declan frowned. "Kids? Who are you talking about?"

"Our children. Jessie and...the twins."

"Twins?" He heard the laughter in her voice and convinced himself she was joking.

"Yes, darling. The twins. I'm pregnant."

"Pregnant? With *twins?* Are you *sure?*"

"As of this morning, I am. I had an ultrasound a couple of hours ago. The doctor happily confirmed it."

Shock surged through him, followed quickly by elation. *"Twins?"*

Chloe's laughter gurgled over the phone. "Yes, darling, we're expecting twins. They're due in a little over six months."

Declan shook his head, still overwhelmed by the news. "You're three months along? How come we didn't know?"

"I don't know. I guess we've both been busy with work and Jessie and everything else that takes up our time. It wasn't like we were trying. I guess it just happened and I wasn't paying that much attention. You are happy about it, aren't you?"

He heard the sudden uncertainty in her voice and hastened to reassure her. "Of course I am! I'm over the moon! I can't wait to tell the others. Are you okay? Have you been sick?"

"A little," Chloe admitted, "but not sick in the way of vomiting. More like dizzy and light headed. It was the reason I went to the doctor."

Declan frowned. "You should have told me about it."

"You've had a lot going on lately. Besides, I didn't think it was too serious. It came and went very quickly and only happened every now and then."

"I wish I could have been there with you at the ultrasound. It's too bad you had to go alone."

"I was sad you couldn't be there, but Savannah came along to keep me company," she said, referring to her good friend. "She and Will are down from Sydney for a few days."

"Hey, that's great. What are they doing in Canberra?"

"Oh, I think Will has some kind of work thing on. He didn't really say. They were booked into a hotel in Civic, but I told them to come and stay here. We have plenty of room for all of them, even little Cole. He's the splitting image of Savannah and as mischievous as a litter of puppies. He and Jessie are getting on like a house on fire."

Declan laughed. "He must have his father's charm. I can't imagine Jessie sharing her toys with anyone."

"That's what I thought, too. We're going to have to watch the two of them over the next decade or so."

A chuckle escaped his lips. "That's if we have the time. With a couple more on the way and Jessie not even two…"

"Yes, we're going to be busy for a while. There's no doubt about it. Lucky I know firsthand how good you are at changing diapers."

He shook his head. "Twins. I still can't believe it."

"You'd better get used to it, Daddy. They'll be here before you know it."

———————

Declan spied the hospital straight up ahead of him and breathed a sigh of relief. It was a fair walk back from the river and he was pleased to see it end. He hadn't noticed the distance when he'd stormed away from Tom earlier, his mind fixed on other things, but now, he picked up his speed. As he crossed the car park and headed toward the entrance, he thought longingly of the hospital's air-conditioned interior.

Tom's rental car was still parked where he'd left it and Declan breathed another sigh of relief. At least he wouldn't be walking home. It was now a little after two, but it was possible Tom was still inside. He might have even caught up with Josie, who'd leaped out of the car in disgust within moments of them coming to a stop.

Not that he could blame her. He'd been a downright idiot. It was time to find his brother and apologize.

Christmas decorations lined the walkway that led into the hospital, reminding him that the season to be merry was right around the corner. A pang went through him at the thought his father might still be in hospital over Christmas. His father loved to celebrate the season like no one else he knew. He could still remember, that as kids, they'd go with their dad and find the biggest Christmas tree around. They'd cart it home in a trailer and then spend the rest of the day decorating it, their dad in charge.

Christmas had always been a time for celebration, a time for families, a time for peace and goodwill on earth. Outsiders might think it was sappy, but it was the way it had always been. Declan only hoped this year would be no different.

His stomach grumbled and he remembered he hadn't had anything to eat since breakfast, not even a coffee. A café, half filled with diners enjoying a late lunch, was immediately off to his right. He walked over to the counter and surveyed a handful of freshly made sandwiches and wraps inside a glass display cabinet.

"I'll have a chicken, lettuce and mayo roll, please and a large cappuccino to go," he told the woman who asked for his order.

"Hey, Declan! Over here!"

Declan turned and spied Tom, Clayton and Josie at one of the round tables. Clayton waved to get his attention. Tom simply looked away.

"I'll be there in a minute." He handed over some money to the woman who'd taken his order and collected his lunch at the end of the counter. A moment later, he joined his siblings.

"Take a seat, mate," Clayton offered, pointing to an empty chair. "Brandon was here a little while ago, but he's gone out to get some fresh air."

Declan nodded his thanks and set his lunch and coffee on the table. He took the empty seat next to Tom. His brother studiously ignored him. Declan cleared his throat. His apology was way overdue.

"I'm sorry for the way I argued with you, Tom. It wasn't right. No matter what anyone else thinks, Dad deserves our loyalty and support. Most especially, mine."

Tom started in surprise and turned to face him. Josie merely shook her head, her eyes wide with disbelief.

"What the hell happened to you while you were outside? Did you have an epiphany, or something?" Josie demanded, frowning.

"No, even better, I had a call from my wife. Let's just say, she made me look at the whole thing a little differently."

Tom shook his head. "Well, whatever she said to you sure changed your attitude. Thank her for me next time you talk to her."

Declan smiled and went to tell them his news. At the last minute, he closed his mouth. He'd wait until he'd told his father. He deserved to be the first one to know. Impatient now to see him, he took a huge bite out of his roll.

"You look like you're in a hurry, mate," Clayton teased. "Easy does it, or you'll be the next one in the hospital. They'll be fishing out lumps of chicken that you've darn well gone and choked on."

"I just want to see Dad. How is he, anyway?" He directed the question to all of them and was met with a variety of shrugs and murmurs.

"He's about the same, as far as we can tell," Tom finally offered. The nurse said he still has some swelling on the brain and he probably won't regain consciousness until it recedes."

"*If* he regains consciousness," Josie added, her expression grim.

"Of course he will," Declan said. "He's Dad. He won't let a little thing like this get him down. Not for long, anyway. Besides, it's Christmas in a few days. We all know how much Dad loves Christmas. Did you notice the lights all over the front porch? He's seventy years old and he's still climbing ladders to hang Christmas lights! There's no way he's going to miss it."

He looked around at his siblings and noted their half-hearted nods of agreement. Dread shivered along his spine and his body went still. "What? What is it? What aren't you telling me?" He looked from one to the other and then swore out loud. "What the hell is going on?"

Tom sighed and clasped his arm. "It's all right, Dec. It's nothing. It's just that..." And he proceeded to warn him about his father's frail appearance.

"He's unwell, Dec," Clayton said quietly. "Prepare yourself. He's really unwell."

Impatience and a wave of urgency surged through him. He had to see his father for himself; make his own judgement about the precariousness of his dad's hold on life. Finishing his coffee in two quick gulps, he pushed his chair away from the table. "Where is he?"

"He's in the ICU. It's on level three," Tom replied.

Declan compressed his lips and nodded and strode toward the elevators.

The caustic smell of disinfectant and cleaning fluid burned Declan's nostrils as he made his way down the corridor to the ICU. Nerves jangled in his belly. After what Clayton had said and the expressions on the faces of Josie and Tom, he was bracing himself for the worst. With a deep breath, he pressed the button to request admission and waited for it to be answered.

A young nurse with a bouncy, blond ponytail and a friendly smile opened the door within moments.

"Oh, hi, I'd like to see Duncan Munro. I'm—"

"His son. I can see how much you resemble your siblings. You all look quite alike. There's been a fair parade of you through here today. It's lovely that your father has so many people who care about him."

"Thank you. Do you think he's up to seeing me?"

"He's resting peacefully at the moment. If you don't stay too long, I'm sure it will be fine. My name's Bridie, by the way." She smiled again and then turned away, throwing over her shoulder, "Follow me and I'll take you to him."

Declan fell into step beside her and kept his gaze averted from the handful of other patients lying in beds along the wall. A moment later, she halted. In the bed lay his father. Declan drew in a sharp breath at the helpless fragility of the man before him.

The tubes and bandages were as his siblings had warned him. A tube protruded from his nose and another one from his arm. Yet another one drained urine to a bag which hung from the side of the bed. The respirator pumped and murmured, along with the flashing green LED lights of the monitors. The ward was otherwise quiet, apart from the whisper of machines attached to the other patients and the soft rubber-soled progress of the staff around the room.

Declan released the breath he wasn't aware he'd been holding and pulled up the chair near the bed. He was glad he'd been warned. It was a shock to see his father like this.

He looked like he was dying.

Immediately forcing the thought away, Declan took his father's hand and held it fast.

"Hello, Dad, it's Declan. How are you doing? You're going to be fine, Dad. Everyone says so. Besides, it's nearly Christmas. We all know how much you love Christmas. You have to get better, Dad and get out of here. Who's going to carve the turkey if you're not home? And what about the home brew we bottled together last time I was home? You told me you were saving it for Christmas. I'm not going to have one without you."

Declan paused and waited for a response, but there was nothing. Trying hard to remain positive, he spoke again. "I have some news, Dad. Chloe's having twins. Can you believe it? I'm still getting used to the idea. I wanted you to be the first to know."

He smiled. "I bet you still remember when Mom told you about Clayton and Riley. I bet you even remember where you were. I know I will. I'll remember the moment forever. I can't wait to tell the others. I'll be bugging Riley to death, asking him a million questions, seeing as he's already been there."

He shook his head and his smile widened on a chuckle. "Twins, Dad! Can you believe it?"

CHAPTER 19

Chanel
Grafton, New South Wales

Chanel watched the passing scenery for a moment or two and then returned her gaze to the road. It had been years since she'd lived in Grafton, but she still knew her way around. There might have been a new building or two and the occasional new apartment block built since she'd left home to attend university in Brisbane, but there were still plenty of familiar landmarks around to guide her to where she was going.

"Take the next left, sweetheart. The hospital's right on the corner."

"Yes, Mom. I haven't been gone that long," she teased and flashed her mother a grin.

A tiny smile tugged at her mother's lips, but it was gone as quickly as it appeared. Chanel bit her lip in concern. Her mother had barely spoken a word to her all day. Apart from telling the others she'd wait until later to visit their father, she'd done nothing but murmur the occasional comment to Chanel's almost endless chatter. It was what she did when she was nervous or upset and ever since the phone call the day before, she'd been feeling a whole lot of both.

She pulled her car into a car park located directly across

from the hospital and switched off the ignition. Gathering her courage, she turned to face her mother.

"What is it, Mom? What aren't you telling me? I get that you're worried about Daddy, we all are. But, there's something else. I've seen you worried before and this isn't it. It's almost like you're sad and mad at the same time. It's not like it's Daddy's fault. I'm sure he didn't plan on bursting a blood vessel."

Her mother sighed heavily and shook her head. "Of course he didn't. It's nothing like that. I don't blame him for becoming ill."

"Then what, Mom? What is it?"

Her mother turned to stare out the passenger side window. She was silent for so long, Chanel didn't think she was going to answer her.

"The police think your father's been having an affair."

Chanel's shocked gasp was loud in the sudden stillness. "*What?* You can't possibly be serious?"

Her mother turned back to face her with eyes that were filled with tears. "Yes, sweetheart, I'm afraid I am." She choked on a sob and covered her face. "I don't believe it, of course, but some of your brothers are struggling with it. I just wanted you to know."

Chanel stared at her, helpless and confused. "Mom, please, I don't understand. How could Daddy be having an affair? You mentioned he was found in a hotel room. You didn't say anything about an affair. Besides, I'm with you. It couldn't possibly be true. We're talking about *Daddy*. I don't believe it. I *won't* believe it. The boys can go to hell," she said a little more forcefully.

Her mother frowned through her tears. "Don't talk like that, Chanel. They're entitled to their opinion. They're just trying to deal with the shock of it. We all are. Don't judge them too harshly. I'm sure once they've had time to think it through, they'll realize it couldn't be true. Besides, I haven't told you everything."

In halting sentences, she told her about what the police had found in the hotel room. Chanel shook her head with increasing vehemence, shock and disbelief warring with her instinctive need to defend the man she loved above all others.

"Daddy would never do anything like that, Mom. I don't care what the police said. You know it as well as I do. There's another explanation. I know there is. As soon as Daddy wakes, he's going to set them straight. You wait and see."

She finished with a fierce frown, not at all sure she wasn't trying to convince herself as much as her mother. No, it couldn't be true. It might have looked that way, but there was no way her father would commit adultery. The mere suggestion of it was beyond absurd.

"Perhaps he was going to surprise you? Perhaps all those things were for *you*? Has anyone considered that? It's nearly Christmas, after all and everyone knows how much Daddy loves to celebrate. Perhaps he was getting into the spirit of things a little early?"

Her mother stared at her and then her mouth tugged up on a smile. Hope lit up her features. "You're right, sweetheart. You're absolutely right. That's what it was. Dad was waiting for *me*. Only, he didn't get to call me before the aneurysm ruptured. Thank you, darling—it makes so much sense. I wish I'd thought of it myself."

"Anytime, Mom. I'm more than happy to help. Let's go inside," she added, her voice soft and full of love. "I really want to see him."

———

Chanel gathered her long hair in her hand and secured it with a hairband. The ponytail hung casually over one shoulder. It was more a style of necessity rather than grace, but it did the trick and kept her hair out of the way. When it was left loose, it had a tendency to fall across her face and she constantly had to brush it away. She didn't want the distraction while she sat with her father.

The elevator stopped at level three and the doors slid

open. She hoisted her handbag over her shoulder and followed her mother out into the corridor. They stopped outside the ICU and Chanel's heart picked up speed. She wanted to see her dad, but she didn't know what to expect. She was terrified she'd look at him and see a stranger.

Don't be ridiculous, she chastised herself. *he's your father, no different to the man you saw when you were home during the Spring Break. He's had an accident, a bleed on the brain. That's all.*

An older nurse with short, dark hair opened the door in response to the buzzer and asked if she could help.

"I'm Marguerite Munro and this is my daughter, Chanel. We'd like to see Duncan Munro."

"Of course, Mrs Munro. You're welcome to visit. At this stage, however, we're still asking that you come in one at a time and that you limit your visit to ten minutes."

"Of course. I understand," her mother replied before turning to look at Chanel. "You go ahead, darling. I'll wait out here."

"No, Mom. You go in first. I don't mind waiting."

"It's okay, sweetheart. I saw him yesterday. I know how much you want to see him. I'll go in after you."

"Are you sure?"

"Yes, of course. You won't be long. I'll go in when you finish."

Chanel looked at her mother closely, but she appeared to be holding herself together. With a little shrug, Chanel leaned over and gave her a quick hug and then followed the nurse into the ward.

The smell was as familiar and comforting as the bedroom her mother still kept for her at home. Being in her final year of med school, Chanel had spent countless hours pounding the corridors during her practical blocks in the hospitals around Brisbane. The feel, the smell, the mood of a hospital never failed to stir her. They were places that ran the whole gamut of emotions: from joy at the birth of a baby to sadness and despair at a death. She loved every minute she spent in them. She couldn't wait until she was working as an intern and calling the sterile, white corridors home.

Of course, it was different when the patient was someone she knew—not only knew, but loved and cherished and adored. Being in a hospital under those circumstances was a world apart from being there in the capacity of a doctor. The thought sobered her. When the nurse came to a halt in front of a bed, Chanel drew in a deep breath.

He looked smaller than she remembered, which was weird. She'd only seen him a couple of months ago. He couldn't have shrunk in that time. She supposed it was because he looked so weak and lifeless, lying still and silent on the bed. Mindful of the bandages that swaddled his head, she stepped closer and pressed a kiss to his cheek, relieved to feel it warm beneath her lips.

"Hi, Daddy," she whispered and then blinked back a rush of tears. This was her *father,* the man who commanded every room he entered. His booming voice could reach from one end to the other and his laughter was just as loud. He was vibrant, charismatic, *alive.* The man on the bed in front of her was anything but.

She'd expected it, of course. She'd seen her fair share of sick people, even seriously ill people, like him. But this was her father. He wasn't just another patient requiring treatment. He wasn't just another patient who might or might not pull through...

With a soft sigh, she dragged the solitary visitor's chair closer to the bed and sat. A moment later, unable to help herself, she stood again and moved to the end of the bed where her father's chart sat in a plastic holder. Flipping it open, she scanned the hospital notes made by the staff on her father's condition.

She was reassured to see his vital signs had remained stable since he'd been brought in by ambulance the day before. His neurological responses were all within normal limits. Although he'd suffered a serious bleed when the artery ruptured, it appeared there were no long-term effects from the emergency and it was expected he'd regain consciousness.

Chanel's shoulders slumped with relief. The notes painted a positive outcome. It seemed there was nothing more to do but wait. Regaining her seat, she reached over and squeezed her father's hand and was a little disappointed when there was no response. She wanted to talk with him. She refused to believe he'd been unfaithful to her mother, but it would be nice for him to open his eyes and confirm it.

Aware that her mother was waiting outside, she stood and leaned over the bed and placed a soft kiss on his forehead. "We're all here for you, Daddy. We're all waiting for you to wake. Get well, Daddy, please. I love you." With a final squeeze of his hand, she left him to his solitude.

CHAPTER 20

Marguerite
Grafton Base Hospital

Marguerite followed the nurse into the ICU and braced herself for what was to come. She'd left the hospital last night, when visiting hours had come to an end and was now apprehensive about what she might find. On her way out, Chanel had reassured her he was doing fine, but nothing changed the fact he was still in a coma and no one could tell her when he might wake up.

Her nursing training told her this wasn't unexpected and didn't necessarily indicate a negative outcome, but this was her husband, the man she'd loved for more than two-thirds of her life. She didn't want vague reassurances or well-meaning platitudes from strangers. She wanted him to open his eyes and smile and tell her he loved her and that no matter what, he'd never, ever cheat on her.

She bit her lip against a fresh surge of emotion and clung to Chanel's suggestion. It made sense. It made perfect sense. And it wasn't the first time. He'd surprised her in the past—not often, but it had happened. She could still remember years ago, when he'd done something similar to celebrate their twenty-fifth anniversary.

It was more than possible he'd been going to do it again. The signs all pointed to it. It made far more sense than the suggestion he was cheating on her. That made no sense at all.

Why else would he be in a hotel room with items so blatantly sexual? Lingerie? Massage oil? A single red rose and champagne? Their wedding anniversary had come and gone months ago. For the first time, he'd forgotten all about it. She'd been too upset to remind him, but could he have been trying to make it up to her? Was he preoccupied with, or seeing another woman...? Or was it merely as Chanel had suggested—an early celebration of Christmas meant for Marguerite and him?

With a sigh, she followed the nurse into the ward. A few moments later, Marguerite spied Duncan where she'd left him. He was still pasty, like he'd been yesterday, but that wasn't surprising. Though it had been years since she'd worked in a hospital, she hadn't forgotten what it looked like to be gravely ill. No one survived a ruptured aneurysm and met you the very next day sitting upright in bed with a smile.

She moved closer and laid her hand against his cheek. Leaning across him, she kissed him softly on the lips and breathed him in. Only the faintest whiff of his cologne teased her nose. Mostly, he smelled like the hospital, the same smell of harsh disinfectant that permeated the temperature-controlled air.

Her fingers slid across his cheek and rasped against his stubble. She'd watched him shave only yesterday morning as she'd been dressing for the day, but already his beard was growing back. Her father had been the same, often grumbling that he needed to shave twice a day to remain looking fresh and presentable.

At the memory, a sad smile tugged her lips slightly upward. She hadn't thought of her father in years. Her parents had been horrified when she'd announced she was marrying Duncan. That seemed like a lifetime ago...

She'd met him late one Saturday night while working in the Emergency Room of a busy Sydney hospital. He'd walked in off the street, bleeding profusely from a nasty gash on his forehead. He'd told her he'd been celebrating at an office Christmas party and had fallen down the stairs. Though she smelled alcohol on his breath, he swore he wasn't drunk.

He'd shot her a crooked smile, his dark chocolate eyes full of mischief. She'd been drawn to him by some invisible force and it had been all she could do to concentrate on cleaning his wound and readying him for the doctor.

When it was time to put the stitches in, he'd asked her to hold his hand. By the time he'd been ready for discharge, she'd fallen head over heels in love. A few months later, Duncan got down on one knee and proposed.

They'd told her parents together. Marguerite had braced herself for a fight. It wasn't that they thought her too young—at twenty-five they were more than happy for her to find a husband and it wasn't that they disapproved of Duncan's job. As a young and ambitious lawyer employed in a prestigious law firm in Sydney, he was more than qualified to support their much-loved, and only daughter.

The problem lay with the color of his skin and the fact that Duncan's parents were aboriginal. His family originated from a small country town in the far west of New South Wales. He'd been born and raised in Bourke and after receiving a scholarship, he'd been sent to boarding school in Sydney.

It was at the prestigious Scot's College where he met and befriended many of the men who would ultimately become influential in his life, including those who supported his upward progress in the law. He was still friends with many of the Old Boys and regularly kept in contact.

But none of that mattered to her parents. They refused to see past his heritage. Their narrow-minded, bigoted attitude infuriated and saddened her, but it didn't change her mind. Three months after Duncan proposed, he told her he'd been offered a job in Grafton. He was to join the partnership of an old established firm, with a view to buying the existing partner out when he retired.

Enjoying the idea of one day having a firm to call his own, he was keen to give it a try. She'd never been out of Sydney, but she was happy to go wherever he chose. All she wanted was to be with him.

They married in a Registry Office in Sydney, a week before they were due to leave. She'd invited her parents, but they'd politely declined. Their regrets had been sent on her mother's personal, gold embossed stationary. They were nothing if not well mannered.

She'd tried not to let their attitude affect her and had been determined to enjoy her day. A couple of nursing friends stood beside her; Duncan had two of his mates from school. They'd celebrated a wedding feast at a local restaurant with plenty of fresh seafood and champagne. Except for the dull ache left by the absence of her parents, she'd never in her life been happier. A month later, after settling in Grafton and finding a house to live, she sent her parents a letter and signed it *Marguerite Munro*. She never heard from them again.

It had been forty years and yet they'd never once tried to contact her. She'd heard through various friends and relatives that they were both still alive and faring well, living in a retirement village not far from where she'd been raised. It saddened her that they'd never known their grandchildren and had missed so much of their lives. Still, it had been their choice. They'd made it clear it was either them or Duncan; she'd never once regretted her decision.

The memory of the hotel room and the things that had been found there intruded into her mind. The tiniest trickle of doubt crept into her heart. *Surely, it couldn't be true?* She couldn't have been betrayed by the man for whom she'd given up so much. He loved her as much as she loved him. He was the moon, she was the stars. They went together like night and day and it had always been that way. It all couldn't be a farce. She simply refused to believe it and yet...

A moan of anguish forced its way up through the tension in her belly. She clenched her jaw and gritted her teeth but the harsh sob persisted. She grasped the hand that lay pale and still on the bedsheet right beside her and held it hard against her cheek. Hot tears ran down her face. As if suddenly giving herself permission, she cried and she cried and she cried.

Her fingers tightened on her husband's in an effort to stem the flood. A movement snagged her attention and she gasped mid-sob. *His fingers had moved! She was sure of it!* She dragged his hand down lower and tightened her fingers again, watching closely for the slightest sign that he felt her hand around his.

And there it was again: The tiniest bending of his fingers. Her sobs came harder and she cried out in relief. Hugging him awkwardly to her, she murmured his name in a litany of pain and love and release.

He was waking up. He really was! He was going to be okay.

———

Duncan fought his way through the weight of thick molasses that held him weighted down. He'd dreamed his baby girl was by his side. He could have sworn he'd heard Chanel's voice, calling to him from afar, but then she was gone and he could only surmise he'd imagined it.

He thought of Marguerite and wondered once again why she hadn't stopped by. Surely, she wasn't one of the doubters? No, it was ridiculous for him to even think that way. She'd never believe he could cheat on her. She was his life. She was his everything, just as he was hers. It had always been that way. For forty years, it had been that way.

His thoughts snagged on Susan and he frowned. In his excitement and haste to get to the hotel, he'd forgotten all about the painting. He stirred restlessly, trying once again to push past the fog.

"Susan...Susan... Must see...Susan."

———

Marguerite's mouth gaped open in shock. She couldn't believe what she'd heard. Not only had Duncan moved his fingers, he'd just gasped another woman's name. Blood rushed through her veins and pounded in her ears. She must have misheard him. Surely he couldn't speak around that tube? She must have been mistaken. *Besides, why would her husband call out another woman's name?*

Fear clawed at her insides and her belly cramped with dread. *Had she been mistaken, after all?* Was Duncan seeing someone else? The thought left her more terrified than when the doctor had told her she had a malignant tumor in her breast. Pain seared her from the inside out and it was all she could do not to cry out. She wanted to escape, to run as far away as she could, but her feet remained frozen in place.

With a desperate gasp, she swiped at her tears and shouted for the nurse. The woman came running and in garbled sentences, Marguerite told her what she'd seen and heard, although she kept the exact words to herself. The next few moments were a blur of movement as doctors and nurses checked vital and neurological signs in an effort to determine if it were true.

At last, Marguerite's legs started moving and she stepped back to keep out of the way of the medical staff to allow them to do their job. She understood that better than most. Dread warred with elation when she thought of what they'd find. She hadn't imagined the movement. Duncan was regaining consciousness.

Within hours, he'd be talking.

Within hours, she'd know the truth.

CHAPTER 21

Duncan
Grafton Base Hospital

Duncan was swimming through treacle, striving hard to move closer to the light. His legs and arms were so heavy, it was like he was barely moving and yet there was an urgency inside him that forced him to keep going. His head felt like he'd been hit by a sledgehammer and his eyes burned with pain. He struggled to open them, but couldn't seem to make them work. He clenched his fists, his jaw, his toes, but it was all too much effort. With a sigh of defeat, he slipped back into the darkness.

He dreamed of Marguerite and how she'd looked the night he met her. Even in her regulation navy nurse's uniform, she was beautiful. Her white blond hair had been pulled back into a bun that sat softly at the back of her neck. A few tendrils had escaped and curled around her face and his fingers had itched to touch them. He stumbled through an explanation as to how he'd come to be injured. He could tell she didn't believe him, but when she smiled, her face lit up like a Christmas tree.

Even in his inebriated state, her eyes looked bluer than the sea. Clear and guileless and innocent, they'd sparkled with life and good humor. She even managed to keep a straight face when he told her he wasn't drunk.

"I might have had one or two," he conceded, "but I really had no choice. It was a Christmas party, after all. What could I do? The partners expected it of me."

She'd lifted one perfectly groomed eyebrow, a couple of shades darker than her hair. "The partners? And who might they be that you felt this...obligation to partake in several libations?"

A smile had tugged at the corners of her full lips and it had been all he could do not to laugh. It was either that or kiss her, and given that they were in the middle of the Emergency Room and she was his treating nurse, he didn't think such a course of action was wise. Or, that she'd appreciate it.

Instead, he explained how he was a lawyer in a rather large firm downtown and that he had a certain...obligation to join with his colleagues in some Christmas cheer. "Just one or two, mind you," he added and had then spoiled it by almost toppling off the bed.

She'd merely smiled and helped him upright, her hands cool and soothing on his heated skin. At the contact, her body stilled too, and he'd forced back a surge of satisfaction: She wasn't as immune to him as she appeared.

When she tilted back his chin for a better look at the gash, he'd cataloged her perfect features. He took the time to savor each one until a blush stole across her cheeks. She dropped her hands and cleared her throat and mumbled something about finding the doctor. It was like the sun moved behind the clouds when she hurriedly walked away.

From the moment she first touched him, blood had flowed to his groin. She left him hard and wanting, made worse by the knowledge there was nothing he could do about it. He wanted her, but more than that, he wanted to *know* her: He wanted to know everything about her. He already knew her name. He'd seen it on her badge: Marguerite Riley, Registered Nurse.

Marguerite. The name rolled off his tongue: rare, exotic, beautiful—just like her.

His brothers would chide him and tell him she was way out

of his league and maybe they'd be right, but he'd always been a fighter and he'd never given up on going after what he wanted. It was one of the reasons he'd done so well in his legal career. He was ambitious and determined and yet still managed to live by his own internal compass: The end didn't always justify the means.

In all his daily dealings, he did his best to live by that creed. Some days, it was easier to do than others, particularly in his role as a defense lawyer. There were times when he despaired at having to front a court room with a defendant he was certain was guilty. Still, he stood and did what he'd been paid to do and did it more than well and told himself it simply wasn't his job to ask the question.

If the prosecutor was inept or too lazy to do his job properly, that was only Duncan's gain—or more precisely, his client's. But as the years went on, even after his move to Grafton, he'd become more and more jaded at the life on the defense's side of the bar table.

After consulting with Marguerite, who was by then his beautiful wife, he'd decided to switch teams. He was in the process of making enquires with the New South Wales Office of the Director of Public Prosecutions about any job vacancies when he was approached by the Attorney General and asked if he would accept an appointment to the bench.

He'd been proud and honored to be nominated and more than a little taken aback. Not only was he a defense lawyer, but he was also an aboriginal. Never before in New South Wales had there been an aboriginal judge in the District Court. He couldn't believe the timing of it. After telephoning Marguerite and receiving her wholehearted blessing, it had taken him all of five minutes to accept.

Apart from proposing to his wife, that had been the best decision of his life. He looked back now, more than thirty years later, and was proud of his judicial time. He'd been a hard judge, but he'd been fair and no one who came before him could argue otherwise. And he'd loved every minute of it. At last, he'd found his purpose: upholding the law he believed in with every ounce of his soul, but applying it with common sense, fairness and justice, in a world where they were often sadly lacking.

The day of his retirement had been met with both sadness and relief. Sadness that a part of his life had ended, but relief that he'd have more time to spend with his family and most of all, with his wife. His years as a lawyer and later a judge had often involved traveling to different circuits and it had meant there were times when he was away from home, sometimes for more than a week.

He'd missed football games, ballet concerts and swimming meets. He'd tried to make it up to them by raising his children to be the best people they could be; by example showing them how to reach for the stars and to never, ever let anything hold them back. And then he missed his wedding anniversary. Well, not exactly *missed it*, rather it had completely slipped his mind.

In all the years since they'd been husband and wife, he'd never forgotten the date. He'd even turned down work if it meant he'd be away on the date he and Marguerite were married. With seven children in the house, they hadn't always been able to get away, but even on the occasions when they'd celebrated at home, it had always been special and full of love. After all these years, she was as beautiful to him as the night they'd met and he loved her even more.

But their last anniversary had gotten caught somewhere in his head. He'd thought about it a fortnight out and had been planning to take her to dinner. Somewhere nice and intimate, where they could enjoy a good meal and fine wine. Perhaps later, they could go dancing, like they had when they were young.

Only, none of it had happened. The day had come and gone. It had been nearly a month later, when he remembered that he'd forgotten.

She hadn't said a word. She'd gone about her day like any other. She hadn't given him a clue. Perhaps, she'd been a little quieter, looking back, he thought she might have been. Perhaps, she'd looked a little sadder, but not enough for him to wonder if something were wrong.

He bit his lip and wished again that she'd said something to remind him about their day. But he'd never needed reminding in the past and that was probably why she'd remained silent.

Had she thought he'd forgotten on purpose? That he'd gone past the point where he cared? Had he been that inattentive? He didn't think so, but then...

Now, he'd gone and ruined it.

CHAPTER 22

Marguerite
Grafton Base Hospital

The young doctor who'd introduced himself as Jordan Holland let Duncan's eyelid drop back into place. He lowered his flashlight and turned to Marguerite with a satisfied smile. "He's coming around, Mrs Munro. Just like we hoped he would."

Relief and elation surged through her and she clasped her hands to her mouth. Her heart thudded so hard she strained to hear his words. The worst was over. Duncan was waking up. *Thank goodness, he was waking up.*

"Do...do you know how long it will be before he opens his eyes and...speaks?" she stammered.

"The signs are all positive for that happening sooner, rather than later. His pupils are reacting equally and I'm very pleased with his other neurological observations. He's reacting to pain and even to simple pressure. You saw his fingers move a little while ago and you even heard him speak. If I were to guess, I'd say it might be within the next hour or two, but it's hard to say for certain. What I will say is that I'm sure he's on the mend. You should be able to talk with him before the day is out."

Marguerite breathed out on a sigh tinged with nervousness. She'd vowed to love and honor him, for better or worse, all the days of her life. She still believed in those vows, made so many years ago, and she would be there for him when he regained consciousness.

"If it's okay, I'll go downstairs and give my family the good news. They've come from all over the place to see him and are very much hoping and praying for the best. I'd like to tell them he's going to pull through."

"Of course," the doctor said, nodding in understanding. "Take your time. Your husband's not going anywhere." He offered her a slight grin. Her return smile felt stiff and unfamiliar. She'd had rare opportunities to smile over the past twenty-four hours.

Despite the fact Duncan had mumbled the name of another woman, she leaned over the bed and kissed him softly on the lips and then pulled slowly away. He didn't react, but she wasn't disappointed. He'd moved his hand. He'd spoken. The doctor was certain he was regaining consciousness. It was more than good enough for her.

She pushed open the door that led into the corridor. The waiting area outside the ICU was empty and she realized Chanel must have gone back downstairs. Hurrying toward the elevators, Marguerite at last let the joy of the doctor's announcement soak all the way through to her bones. While the fear of what she'd discover when her husband finally spoke didn't dissipate, the sheer relief that he was going to be okay overwhelmed her. Her smile returned and slowly widened into a huge grin. She couldn't wait to tell her children.

———————

Tom was the first one to notice her. He was holding a cup of coffee halfway to his mouth when he spied her coming toward them. Clayton, Josie, Riley, Declan and Chanel were all seated at the table with him, so engrossed in conversation they didn't notice her approach. Brandon was on the phone and stood a little distance from the table, his back half turned away from them.

Tom set his cup down and half stood. "What is it, Mom? What's happened?"

She drew in a breath and opened her mouth. "It's Dad. He's-he's...waking up. He's going to be all right." Her voice hitched. Tears burned. She swallowed the lump in her throat and cleared it, her voice hoarse. "They're optimistic he's going to be all right."

Chairs scraped across linoleum. Amid smiles and cries of relief, she was engulfed in hugs from every direction.

"Mom, that's fantastic!"

"Have you spoken to him?"

"When can we see him?"

The questions came from her in a babble of noise and confusion. She shook her head and held up her arms in an effort to quiet them down, like she used to when they were young.

"Children, please, one at a time. I can't even hear myself think." She softened the order with a smile and pulled the nearest one close. Chanel returned the embrace and hugged her tightly. Her youngest daughter looked up at her, beaming.

"It's wonderful news, Mom. What did the doctor say?" The others stood close by, watching her expectantly.

"Your father moved his fingers and then he murmured a couple of words. I called for the nurse who got the doctor who examined him closely and then told me he was regaining consciousness."

"I can't believe Dad spoke," Tom said. "What did he say?"

Marguerite shrugged and looked away. "Nothing important. He didn't even make sense, but at least he said something. It's a good sign. The doctor said it might be another hour or two before he's conscious again."

"Wow," Josie added. "I can't wait to tell him hello."

"Me, either," Declan said softly, his expression fierce.

Brandon turned to face them with an eyebrow raised in silent query. He still had the phone to his ear.

"Dad's waking up," Clayton mouthed. Brandon frowned with incomprehension.

"Oh, for Christ's sake," Tom exploded. "Get off the phone! Dad's waking up!"

Brandon's eyes widened in shock. A moment later, he ended his call. His gaze moved from one sibling to another until it finally landed on his mother. "Dad's waking up? Is it true?"

She nodded and smiled through her tears. "Yes, darling. He is."

"Whoop! That's fantastic news! I can't wait to tell Alex. *Alex!* I almost forgot. She's gone into labor. She's called Lily who's on her way over. She'll drive her to the hospital. I-I have to go, Mom. I have to go and be with Alex."

Marguerite's heart beat a little faster in excitement at the thought of the impending arrival. "Of course, Brandon. Go. Your wife needs you. Dad will be fine. It might be a few hours before he's fully conscious. By that time, you could be back in Sydney."

"Yes, I've had a list of flights on standby ever since I arrived." He checked his watch. "The next one leaves in a little under an hour."

"I can drive you to the airport," Clayton offered.

"That would be great, Clay. I'd really appreciate it."

"No problem, Bran. I wouldn't want you to miss the birth." When Clayton spoke again, his voice was thick with emotion. "There's something indescribable about being present when your children are born. It's a moment you never forget."

Brandon nodded. "Yeah, and with Alex having such a hard time of it with Bella, I can't bear the thought of not being there to support her."

He stepped forward and gave Marguerite a fierce hug. She returned it with an equal amount of enthusiasm. "Go and be with your wife, son and give her our love and best wishes. We'll be thinking of you both and waiting to hear the good news."

"Thanks, Mom. Let's hope everything works out that way."

"You have to think positive, Brandon. Take a look at your father. A little while ago, none of us knew what to expect or whether we'd ever get to speak with him again. Now, he's waking up. Miracles happen, son. You just have to believe."

"Oh, I believe in them, all right," Brandon replied, his voice catching. "It was a miracle Alex and I ever got back together, let alone that we have two more children." He pulled away from her. "I need to go to her, Mom. I need to be with my family."

He turned on his heel and threw a glance in Clayton's direction. "You ready?"

"Stay safe, Brandon," she called out to his retreating form. He lifted a hand to acknowledge he'd heard and her shoulders slumped on a soft sigh.

"They'll be fine, Mom. Alex will be, too." Josie offered the words of comfort and Marguerite nodded gratefully.

"Of course they will. I'm just being silly. It must have something to do with all the emotions we've had to deal with over the past twenty-four hours. I'm suddenly quite exhausted."

Chanel's eyes immediately clouded with concern. "Come and sit down, Mom. Have a coffee. Have you even eaten today?"

She let herself be led with a daughter on either side and took comfort from their gentle ministrations. She couldn't wait to talk to Duncan and sort things out once and for all. Then her life could return to normal. The thought that things might never be normal again intruded sharply, but she forcefully pushed it aside. Duncan hadn't been having an affair. She simply flat-out refused to believe it.

And that was that.

CHAPTER 23

Duncan
Grafton Base Hospital

The second time Duncan struggled to return to the light that beckoned him, he was a little more successful. Some of the pain in his head had receded and the weight on his chest was slightly more bearable. Determined to reach his goal, he tried to take a deep breath, intent on pushing through whatever he had to in order to come out on the other side.

Instead, he choked and coughed and spluttered and gasped. There was something in his throat, something obstructing his breathing. Hands reached for him, holding his face and body while he thrashed his head from side to side, trying to rid himself of whatever it was that was blocking his path to the light.

"It's all right, Mr Munro. Take it easy. I'm Doctor Jordan Holland. I've been looking after you. You've been on a respirator. Lie still, while we remove it." The calming voice registered through the fog that clouded his brain. He concentrated on the words and at last understood. He was in a hospital. He had a breathing tube stuck down his throat. Surrendering to the efficient ministrations of the people working over him, he sighed in relief when the tube was eventually removed.

"There you go. I'm sure that feels better."

Duncan squinted into the light he'd been so desperate to reach and caught the hazy image of a young man in a white lab coat hovering above him. Duncan nodded and tried to speak, but his mouth was so dry, all he could manage was a croak.

"It's okay," the man he presumed to be a doctor said. "Take your time. You've been through a bit of an ordeal. We're glad to have you back with us."

Duncan frowned and tried to remember what had happened. The hotel room and his reason for being there slowly came back to him. He'd gone to so much trouble to make sure everything was perfect. He'd brought everything they needed and a little more. He'd been beside himself with excitement at the thought of showing her the necklace. He'd been just about to call his wife when the room had tilted and his world had gone black.

Marguerite! Where was she? He needed to see her. He needed to explain. He could only imagine what she thought...

"H-how long?" he rasped, trying his best to keep the doctor in focus.

"How long have you been unconscious?"

Duncan nodded.

"About twenty-four hours, we think. You were unconscious when a staff member from the hotel found you. The police and the ambulance were called and then you were transported here. It's now—" He glanced at his watch. "A little after three."

Twenty-four hours. He felt a fresh wave of nervous desperation. He had to see his wife. He had to talk to his family. He drew in a cautious breath and eased it out. He opened his mouth again and then closed it and cleared his throat, grimacing at the soreness.

"M-my wife," he managed. "Where is she? I need to see her."

The doctor nodded and smiled and leaned over to pat his hand. "Of course, Mr Munro. She was right here. I'll have someone take a look outside and see if they can find her. You've had plenty of visitors. All seven of your children have been here, so I've been told. You're very lucky to have such a loving family."

Duncan wondered at the doctor's wistful tone but soon dismissed it and focused his thoughts on his family. The knowledge that he hadn't dreamed their presence by his bedside warmed his heart. At the same time, dread crept through his veins. He wasn't sure which of them thought him guilty of adultery. He only hoped one of them wasn't Marguerite.

Renewed urgency rushed through him and he struggled to sit up. He grabbed for the bedrails and tried to gain enough leverage to lift his head and shoulders off the bed. "Please," he gasped. "I need to see my wife."

"*Shh, it's okay, Mr Munro. Someone's gone to find her.*" This time, it was a pretty blond nurse who spoke gently to him. "You've only just come out of a coma. We'll raise the head of your bed so that you can see a little better. We don't want you sitting too far up at the moment—and especially not unsupported. You may still feel slightly dizzy and maybe even a little nauseous if we rush things."

Duncan slumped back against the pillows and sighed. The effort had worn him out. He grimaced in annoyance and pain. He'd been out cold for only a day and he felt as weak as a day-old kitten. He wasn't used to feeling so helpless, so dependent upon those around him. If his head wasn't pounding like an orchestra of kettle drums he'd have been as irritated as hell.

The nurse with the kind blue eyes must have noticed his expression. She leaned down, close to his face and rested her hand on his arm. Her touch was cool and calming on his skin.

"Would you like me to get you something for the pain or an ice cube for your throat, Mr Munro?"

The compassion in her voice brought tears to his eyes. He bit his lip and nodded. He hated feeling so feeble, but at that moment it was all he could do not to sob from the pain.

"It's my head. It's...it's agony. But, please don't knock me out again," he begged. "I need to speak with my wife."

"Of course," the nurse smiled with understanding. "You've only just woken. We don't want to put you back to sleep again."

"Thank you," he whispered and closed his eyes, not even caring that the tears now rolled silently down his cheeks.

"I'll be back as soon as I can," the nurse replied and disappeared from his sight. Duncan sighed and closed his eyes...and waited.

CHAPTER 24

Marguerite
Grafton Base Hospital

Now that the moment was upon her, Marguerite didn't know whether she wanted to run and hide or demand to hear the truth from her husband. She was back to feeling terribly unsure what his words would reveal, and the uncertainty of the outcome was tearing her up inside.

A nurse had found her in the lobby where she'd been listening to the sound of carolers. A small group of men and women were singing Christmas carols, their faces angelically immersed in the beautiful hymns. Marguerite had heard them from the café where she'd been seated with her children. She'd pushed away from the table and moved toward the sound, their music stirring deep inside her soul.

She'd always loved Christmas. It was her favorite time of the year. She didn't need a therapist to tell her the reason. It had everything to do with her husband. He was her life... He was her everything. She couldn't bear the thought that he might have been unfaithful; she prayed in quiet desperation that she wouldn't find out there was someone else...

A nurse had touched her gently on the elbow and murmured the words she'd been longing to hear: Her husband was awake and he was asking for her.

Even now, after relaying the good news to her children and heading toward the elevators, the nurse's words kept bouncing inside her head: *He was asking for her.*

Surely, that was a good sign? Surely, that could only mean he still loved her as deeply as he always had? He wouldn't be asking for her if his conscience wasn't clear. *Would he?*

She sighed impatiently and shook her head, doing her best to keep those thoughts at bay. They were doing nothing but filling her head with confusion and second-guesses. Regardless, Duncan was awake. It was time she learned the truth.

She came to a halt outside the all-to-familiar doors that led into the ICU. With another fortifying breath filling her lungs, she squared her shoulders and pressed the buzzer that would gain her entry. The next few minutes passed in a blur. She was ushered into the hospital ward by a nurse with a wide white grin.

Barely aware of her feet moving, Marguerite followed the girl again and stopped at her husband's bedside. His bed had been raised, allowing him to recline against the pillows. The tube in his mouth had been removed, along with the one in his nose. His eyes were closed, but his color had returned and all at once, she was dizzy with relief.

He was alive and he was going to get better. He was breathing on his own. He looked like the husband she'd loved for so long, no longer a man balancing between life and death. She took his hand and pressed it to her lips and tried to still her trembling. Tears filled her eyes and she let them fall. She gasped on a sob and then gasped again when he opened his eyes and stared at her.

"*Marguerite.*" His voice was so scratchy, she barely heard him, but then he said it again.

With a cry of joy, she leaned over the bedrail and embraced him a little awkwardly. The strong, sure beat of his heart thumped reassuringly beneath her ear. He still needed a shave and he still smelled of hospital, but he was hers and he was awake. Slowly, she lifted her head and moved away from him. The chair she'd vacated earlier was where she'd left it and she eased herself down onto it.

Duncan turned his head in her direction, his gaze dark and shadowed. "I'm sorry," he rasped. "I'm so sorry."

Her heart stopped cold and her body filled with dread. She shook her head in wordless denial. All of a sudden, her courage deserted her and she prayed that he'd say nothing: She simply didn't want to know.

As if sensing her distress, Duncan's eyes grew more desperate. "Please, I need to tell you. I need to explain."

"Who's Susan?" The words fell out before she realized it. Wishing she could cover her ears but knowing she couldn't, she clenched her jaw and braced herself against what was to come.

Duncan merely frowned at her, his eyes shadowed and confused. "Did the police tell you where they found me?"

She shook her head no and caught the flash of relief in his chocolate eyes. Anger stirred low in her belly. "Riley did."

The relief in his gaze dissipated and the tension increased around his mouth. "What did he tell you?"

She compressed her lips, suddenly wanting it over with. "You haven't answered my question. Who in heaven's name is Susan and why were you waiting for her in a hotel room?"

He closed his eyes and his shoulders slumped. With every moment that it took him to answer, her anger grew. Her chest tightened. Heat crept up her neck.

"Susan is an artist and it wasn't her I was waiting for. I was waiting for you."

His reply was so quiet, she wasn't sure she'd heard it correctly. "But you called out her name. You said you had to see her." She suddenly registered what he'd said. "What is her being an artist got to do with anything? How do you think I've been feeling, knowing half of Grafton knows my husband was cheat—"

"*No!*" The word seemed to be wrenched from deep inside him. His eyes were filled with pain. He gripped his head with his hands, as if that could somehow relieve it. "That's not how it was. It was meant to be a surprise. I-I'd forgotten our anniversary and I wanted to make it up to you. I'd been planning it for weeks. I'd bought all those things in secret, I'd even booked the room. All that was missing was you."

Marguerite stared at him, disbelief warring with an ever-increasing hope. *Had* he planned it all for her? She stood and moved closer to the bed and searched his face for the truth. He held her gaze without flinching. Tears ran down his cheeks.

"I was just about to call you," he continued hoarsely. "Everything was perfect, just like I'd imagined it. I couldn't wait to see you and watch the surprise on your face. You were so sad when I forgot our anniversary. I'll never forgive myself for causing you such pain. I wanted to give you a memory that would wipe out the awful one; a memory you would cherish forever."

A sob caught in her throat. It was just as she'd hoped. He hadn't been unfaithful. He'd been trying to show her how much he loved her and how sorry he was for causing her distress. He loved her. He'd always loved her. Just like she'd always loved him.

Her heart flooded with emotion and she could no longer speak. She sobbed against his strong, broad chest and cried tears of joy and happiness and relief.

His arms came up around her and held her as best he could. She thought of their children and knew she must go and tell them. They were nursing their own private pain with the unknown hanging above them, like a toxic cloud of nuclear waste. Any moment, it could fall and cover them and their lives would never be the same again.

But it hadn't happened. It wasn't true. Their father wasn't an adulterer. He hadn't cheated on his wife. He was the man they'd always looked up to, respected, admired and loved. He was the man who'd inspired them, encouraged them and helped them along the way. He was Duncan Munro: her husband; their father; her love.

Epilogue

Duncan
Grafton, New South Wales
Christmas Day

The delighted squeals of the children sent a surge of joy straight to Duncan's heart. Riley's twins, Rosie and Daisy, chased after one another around the living room with dolls and spades and sand buckets clutched beneath their arms. Their parents shook their heads in exasperation and asked for them to stop, but to little avail.

Brandon and Alex snuggled on the couch, their three-day-old baby son, Justin, cradled lovingly in their arms. Their daughter, Bella, sat at their feet, engrossed in a new toy that rattled and rolled and played music.

Chloe returned from yet another trip to the bathroom looking pale and drawn. It might have been Christmas Day and she might have been three months along, but her morning sickness hadn't let up and was beginning to take its toll. She took her seat beside Declan and Jessie and offered her husband a shrug and a tiny smile. Declan pulled his wife close and pressed a loving kiss on her forehead.

Tom and Lily sat together at the other end of the couch. With their fingers entwined, they murmured and softly laughed while they watched the younger children play. Cassie and Joe had gone outside, enthralled with their

Christmas gifts. For Joe, it was an iPad and for Cassie, a new smart phone.

Clayton and Ellie stood off to one side, their faces taut and distant. Duncan sighed inwardly and hoped they'd work things out. He'd tried to talk to his son earlier, when he'd noticed the obvious strain between Clayton and his wife, but Clayton had brushed his efforts aside and Duncan backed away. He respected their need for privacy and to sort out their problems on their own. He only prayed there wouldn't be lasting damage; the kind that never heals.

Olivia had removed herself from the gathering as soon as the gift giving had finished. He hadn't failed to notice she'd only thanked her father. Of course, the boys had more than made up for her lack of exuberance. Mitchell and Damon had almost bowled Ellie over in their enthusiasm to show their mother what Santa had left for them under the tree. She'd smiled and hugged both of them close, but Duncan had caught the sparkle of tears in her eyes. The sight broke his heart.

He stirred from his position in his favorite armchair and the girls at his feet turned as one, identical expressions of concern on their faces.

"Are you all right, Dad?" asked Josie.

"Can I get you anything, Daddy?" asked Chanel.

He leaned forward and ruffled their hair with his hand, like he used to when they were young. "No, thank you, sweetheart," he said to his youngest and then turned his gaze on Josie.

"I'm fine, darling, but I think all that gift giving has worn me out. Not to mention the huge portion of Christmas lunch I consumed. I think I might go upstairs."

Josie smiled. "Okay, Dad. Are you sure you don't need anything?"

He looked across at his wife who stood on the other side of the room. She was untangling a toy fishing line from the hair of one of Clayton's sons. The boy's brother looked on nearby, trying desperately to hide his guilt. Duncan covered his mouth to contain a chuckle.

As if she sensed his gaze, Marguerite looked up and smiled. His heart thumped hard with emotion.

God, he loved her.

He raised an eyebrow and indicated the stairs with his head. Her smile widened and her eyes sparkled with sudden mischief. He pushed himself upright and his daughters moved out of the way. Suddenly eager to get to the bedroom, he made haste across the living room floor.

"I'm taking a nap," he muttered to anyone who cared to listen.

He'd barely turned down the bed when he heard her open the door. She closed it silently behind her and swung slowly around to face him. She stared at him with eyes that were already shadowed with desire. The familiar spark surged through him. After all these years, he still wanted her.

"It's not too soon, is it?" she asked.

"No, the doctor cleared me for gentle exercise yesterday morning and then he wished me a Merry Christmas."

She smiled and her eyes teased him. "I guess I can be gentle." With tender fingers, she touched the wound on the side of his head. The bandages had been removed before he'd been discharged, but the incision had been covered with a dressing. Marguerite had been given the job of cleaning it twice a day with Betadine and peroxide.

She stepped back and he watched while she undid the buttons of her blouse of Christmas red. It fell from her shoulders. Her straight, fitted skirt soon followed. She stood before him, proud and beautiful, in nothing but her underwear.

He moved to the dresser and opened the top drawer. Reaching inside, he pulled out the red velvet jeweller's box. The police had recovered it from the hotel and had given it to him, along with the suitcase of other things. The constable who had handed it to him had blushed to the roots of his hair. Duncan had refrained from making a comment.

He came up behind his wife and put his hands on her shoulders, pressing his lips against the silkiness of her bare skin. She shivered under his attentions and his body stirred in anticipation.

"I have a gift for you," he murmured between kisses.

"Mm?" she murmured and moved her head to give him greater access to her neck.

He kissed her again and then withdrew. She turned slowly to face him. He held the necklace in both hands. "Happy anniversary," he whispered.

Her eyes went wide. "Duncan, it's beautiful. Where ever did you find it?" She reached for it and he laid it flat against his palm.

"In a jeweller's store up the coast. It reminded me of you the moment I saw it. The diamonds remind me of your sparkle and light. The rubies remind me of your lips. The sapphires remind me of your beautiful eyes and then there's the heavy gold chain. It reminds me of the color of your hair and your skin in the summer sun—and the price of it..." He winked at her and smiled. "The price of it reminds me that no money could buy what you've given me over the years. Your value can never be measured."

By the end of his little speech, she had her hands up to her mouth and tears sparkled in her eyes.

"Hey," he protested gently, "I didn't mean to make you cry."

"They're tears of joy," she whispered and kissed him softly on the lips.

"I'm glad, because I haven't finished yet." He went over to the closet. Pulling open the door, he retrieved the second gift he'd stowed there. "Merry Christmas, my darling."

"What is it?"

"You'll have to open it."

Carefully, she unwrapped the large present and then gasped when she saw what it was. A painting of the two of them as they'd been not long after they'd married. Young and just as in love as they were now.

"I commissioned Susan to paint it. I meant to collect it the day I fell ill. I guess that's why it was playing on my mind; why I mentioned Susan's name in the hospital. I was concerned I'd forgotten to get it. I didn't want it to go missing."

"Oh, Duncan, it's beautiful. I love it!" She leaned close and offered him a kiss.

"I'm glad," he murmured and kissed her back.

The kiss turned heated and his lips moved over hers. Pulling away, he undid the clasp of the necklace and fixed it around her neck before taking her back in his arms. He slanted his mouth against hers and deepened the kiss, loving the feel of her. She tasted of brandy and Christmas pudding and custard. She tasted of love.

With increasing urgency, his hands went to his polo shirt and he dragged it over his head. His shorts followed. Glancing across the room, he spied the windows and cursed beneath his breath. Striding across the room, he drew the drapes against the summer heat and flicked the thermostat on the cooler to low.

Marguerite's hands went around her back and she fumbled with the clasp of her bra.

"Here, let me," he murmured and brushed her fingers aside.

The lacy, black undergarment fell to the carpet and joined the growing pile of clothes. His hands went immediately to her breasts and he sighed in contentment. He bent his head and pressed kisses across her chest.

"You're so beautiful," he whispered.

She blushed and looked away. "I'm sixty-five years old."

"Twenty-five. Sixty-five. Ninety-five. Age is just a number. It's what's in here that counts." He pressed a hand to his heart. "You'll always be the girl that I married and I'll love you until I die."

She put her arms around him and her eyes filled with love. "You're my one and only, Duncan. You're my love. You're my life."

He pulled her closer and rested his cheek on the top of her head, breathing in the sweet scent of her hair. As tall as she was, he was taller and she fit neatly under the crook of his arm. It had always been that way and it always would be.

'Til death do we part.

Note to Readers

I do hope you have enjoyed reading Duncan and Marguerite's story. Please feel free to leave a review for The Christmas Vigil. Every review is appreciated and really helps a new author like me.

The Ransom—Book Seven in the Munro Family Series is the next book in the Munro Family Series and is Lane and Zara's story.

Here's a sneak peek:

When Ellie Cooper married Clayton Munro, she was hopeful his daughter, Olivia would accept her into her life. Six years later, despite all of Ellie's efforts, the ten-year-old continues to reject her at every turn. Then Olivia goes missing while in Ellie's care...

Detective Senior Sergeant **Lane Black** *of the New South Wales State Crime Command catches the case. A child is missing, presumed kidnapped and time is of the essence. To complicate matters, the State Attorney General's youngest daughter was present at the time of the kidnapping. The girls look very alike. Could it be a case of mistaken identity?*

When the Attorney General, David Dowton, is told his daughter's best friend has been kidnapped, he's immediately assailed with guilt. He knows the abduction has nothing to do with his daughter or her friend. He agonizes over what to tell the police. He certainly can't tell them the truth.

*When Lane interviews David, his suspicions are aroused. Why is the man so nervous? David's oldest daughter, **Zara**, is also on edge. Immediately drawn to her exotic beauty, Lane does his best to remain unmoved and impartial. A child is missing. He needs to put together the pieces to find her before it's too late.*

Will the Dowtons cooperate with his investigation? What are they hiding...and why?

The Ransom will be released on 5 January, 2015 and is AVAILABLE NOW for pre-order from your favorite retailer.

About the Author

Chris Taylor grew up on a farm in north-west New South Wales, Australia. She always had a thirst for stories and recalls writing her first book at the ripe old age of eight. Always a lover of romance and happily-ever-afters, a career in criminal law sparked her interest in intrigue and suspense. For Chris to be able to combine romance with suspense in her books is a dream come true.

Chris is married to Linden and is the mother of five children. If not behind her computer, you can find her doing the school run, taxiing children to swimming lessons, football, ballet and cricket. In her spare time, Chris loves to read her favorite authors who include Richard North Patterson, Sandra Brown, Kathleen E Woodiwiss and Jude Devereaux.

You can find out more about Chris and sign up for her newsletter at her website:

http://www.christaylorauthor.com.au